I0690565

WE HAVE JUST LANDED
VOLUME TWO

First Edition

Published by The Nazca Plains Corporation
Las Vegas, Nevada
2010

ISBN: 978-1-61098-015-9
E-book: 978-1-61098-016-6

Published by

The Nazca Plains Corporation ®
4640 Paradise Rd, Suite 141
Las Vegas NV 89109-8000

PUBLISHER'S NOTE
We Have Just Landed is a work of fiction created wholly by *Wade Wright*'s imagination. All characters are fictional and any resemblance to any persons living or deceased is purely by accident. No portion of this book reflects any real person or events.

Cover Design, Ian Ray
Art Director, Blake Stephens

DEDICATION

To each and every individual, man or woman, gay or straight, that has successfully found his or her true love!

WE HAVE JUST LANDED
VOLUME TWO

First Edition

Wade Wright

CONTENTS

PREFACE

Cory, a hot and hunky twenty six year old, that stood about six foot two, and weighed in at about a hundred and seventy five pounds, and Jimmy, a six foot one, twenty eight year old, one hundred and ninety pounder, had a most unusual meeting – all based on the quick sighting of one pair of some very hot looking, form fitting, and tight 501s! Additionally, some rather unusual ways of meeting each other helped them each realize, very quickly, that they had each "finally found his man."

All during the very short time of just one weekend, their finding each other – some very unusual circumstances happening all at the right time – and the realization that their sexual desires were all in perfect alignment – sealed the deal! They were definitely meant for each other! Each man realized that some funny "super natural power" had taken control of them, and it had been the overpowering force that had brought the two of them together. They accepted that they were true sole mates, and were truly intended to be together.

CHAPTER 1

Breakfast in the Morning

Cory was up a little earlier than Jimmy was, and was in the process of picking up some of the clothes that had been flung around the room the night before. He was attempting to be quiet, but apparently had not managed that quite enough. Noticing that Jimmy was lying there watching him go about his housely duties, he then stopped, went over to the bed, sat down on the edge of it and jokingly asked, "Well just who do 'you' happen to be? Where did I find 'you'? Are there some funny things from last night that I just don't happen to remember about? Did I bring you home just for the evening and some bedroom fun, or did I declare the rest of my life to you, young man?"

"Well sir," Jimmy jokingly responded, "I'm just not so sure who in the hell you are either, but yes – you did bring me home for some bedroom fun last night, and damn good fun it was! You found me in the alley, and yes you did declare the rest of your entire life to me!"

Laughing and at the same time lying down so that his body would lie completely across Jimmy's torso, Cory said, "Oh yes! I do remember last night now! Feeling that thing under me definitely reminds me of last night! I kind of remember something like somebody putting a telephone pole up in my ass, and I kind of remember that it was right after getting that up in there, and securely placed, that was when I declared the rest of my life to you. Hell, I probably did that since I wasn't sure if I'd ever be able to get that damn big pole out of me or not! I probably figured that I was going to have you up in my ass, the rest of my life."

"Yeah, man! It was up there, and if you lie across me and rub your body up against it anymore this morning, it's going to go right back up in there again! With you lying across it, I can tell, it is getting itself ready!"

"You don't need to tell me that! From just lying on it, I can feel it doubling in size! Shit, I still cannot believe how damn big that thing will get! It starts out so small, well maybe not so small, but at least normal size, and then it just keeps getting bigger and bigger and bigger! Not right now baby, cause we've got things to do, but you are going to fuck my tiny little ass with that damn big thing again later today! Okay?"

"So what we got to do right now?"

"Breakfast, my man, breakfast! I've already made some fresh orange juice, gotten some eggs ready to put on the stove and have placed a new flower on the table especially for you – to show you –that – well, even though I may not know where in the hell I found you, why you are here, or if I've committed my entire life to you or not – I kind of think you are a special type of person, and I want our first breakfast together to be a pretty one. So I did my gardening this morning. I picked one rose, and it is waiting for you on the table. The Sunday paper is waiting for you also! Now you can look at the paper while I finish breakfast, but once we're at the table, you have to put the paper down. I certainly do not intend to start out, on our very first morning, by looking across the table and looking at a newspaper, when I want to see your pretty face, okay? Now, get your ass up out of bed, grab a quick shower and come to the kitchen. Okay?" Cory said, as he leaned forward toward Jimmy and gave him a solid kiss on the forehead.

"Yes Sir! Yes Sir! Wow, the first day and I'm being ordered to get out of bed! I don't know if this is a good thing or not!" Jimmy looked at Cory, grinned and asked, "Will I ever be able to sleep in if I want to?" Jimmy's realization of what was being said was almost too exciting for him! The, 'I want our first breakfast together to be a pretty one' and then the, 'I certainly do not intend to start out on our very first morning,' were comments that had the kind of words in them that he really wanted to hear. Cory was definitely talking in long-term, terms!

"Yeah, you will get to sleep in sometime, but not until I get tired of you and don't want to be around you in the morning, but that sure as hell is not today! We are not going to lose any time today by sleeping when we could be doing stuff together. Hey, the way I see it, we went to sleep last night, what about 2:30 and now it's 8:30? Well, as I see it, even though maybe I had my hands on you that whole time, I feel like I have already lost about 6 hours of being with you, since I was unconscious. When you get your little butt, and that damn big enormous dick of yours out of bed, there is a clean blue towel and wash rag for you in that bathroom. And you will notice, if you look, I have emptied out the top drawer on the left side of the cabinet so that you can put your toothbrush and stuff in there and know where it is! Oh, and you just might happen to find a small picture of me in that same drawer. If that picture is there after you have had a chance to remove it, I will be damn mad, because that picture is for you to put in your billfold. Then you can look at me anytime you wish! Understand, man? In other words, you had better act excited that I want you to carry my picture! Okay? Understand?"

"Yeah, oh, yes man! I understand! How did you know that I have a mouse in my house and I needed a scary picture?" Jimmy strongly, and laughingly asked.

"Oh shit, damn you! I could just slap the hell out of you," Cory laughed as he kind of swung his hand at Jimmy as if to attempt a slap.

"You get your ass out of bed! I'm going out to the kitchen and finish breakfast. Now don't take too long in the shower. You don't need to be playing with yourself while showering. I'll do that for you later. Is whole wheat bread okay for you, for toast?"

"Yeah, that sounds good."

"Is scrambled eggs okay?"

"Hey how can a man say no? Sounds very good to me! I'll only take a couple of minutes in the shower, and then I'll be right out. You've only got gym shorts on. Should I just put on some shorts, or should I get more dressed for someplace else? I don't know what we're doing – so darling – my little tight asshole darling – how should I get dressed? God, your ass was so damn good and so damn tight, last night!"

"Hey don't you call me a tight asshole. That asshole has had a lot of big stuff up in it, and if your dick was not so damn big, then it wouldn't be such a tight hole. When something big goes into something not quite as big, it's gonna be tight!"

"Oh, okay then. I'll never tell any of the guys that you have a tight asshole. I'll tell 'em that it is a big, loose and sloppy asshole! Right?"

"Shit man, I simply cannot win with you! We just won't talk about my asshole to anybody then, okay? Get your ass up and just put on some shorts. We'll decide what we're gonna do after breakfast. Go through the stuff in that dresser and see if you can find a pair of shorts that's big enough for you, just in case you get a hard-on. Okay, man?"

"Oh, am I supposed to look for a pair of shorts that have a big baggy front in them? Well that certainly does sound different, maybe not so attractive, but different."

"Get your ass out of bed, I'm going to the kitchen!"

Just as Cory was finishing the toast and the scrambled eggs, Jimmy came down the hall and entered the kitchen. "Wow!" He exclaimed. "How long have you been up? The kitchen certainly did not look like this last night when we went to bed! The table is beautiful! Cory, breakfast just cannot be like this everyday, man. This is way too much! Is the rose out of your yard? I hope you didn't steal it from somebody else's yard."

"No, I did not steal it! I've got a small flower bed out back. Having a rose bush, just happened to pay off very nicely this morning. No, breakfast will not always be this fancy, but I look at today as being quite different and very special. To me anyway!"

"And it is to me also!" Jimmy said, as he put his arms around Cory and took him up close to himself and placed a good firm kiss on Cory's lips.

"I think you and I are certainly walking the same road here, and I think maybe we have a lot of talking to do so that we completely understand each other. I mean, it's not yet been twenty-four hours since we met each other, and I kind of think we both feel like something greater than ourselves was involved. Right?"

"Yes, you really are right! Something kind of took over both of our lives yesterday, and although I may not understand it, I've heard before that funny things like this has happened to other guys in the past, but I sure never expected to be one of 'em. Yeah, let's eat. Then maybe we can go for a walk over by the lake and talk. Okay?"

"Sounds like a game plan to me! What can I do here? Is everything ready? Oh, wait, let me pour the orange juice. Are these the glasses for the juice?"

Breakfast was very enjoyable for both of the men, and small talk about the night before was the main conversation until the phone rang. Cory answered it and Jimmy was within very clear ear shot.

"Hello, this is Cory. Oh, hi David! Uh – well – yeah – I would say very, very well! I guess the best way to answer that is to tell you that all of the guys at the Calf's Skin now know him, and I just found out that he has to be told about five times to get up in the morning, and that breakfast is ready. Yeah, he is! He's here and listening to me. No, I mean get up out of bed, no, not that kind of 'get up.' He has no problem with that type of 'get up!' He's waving at the phone as to tell you hello. Jimmy, David says 'Hi' back to you. Okay man. I'll talk to you later, but I'm not so sure exactly when it'll be. Okay? Tell Suzie that Jimmy and I said 'Hi,' okay? Yeah, I'll talk to you later. Bye."

As Cory turned back to Jimmy, "He called to see how yesterday's lunch turned out. He was wondering why I had not called him. I guess he now knows! He commented that lunch must have gotten a little lengthily! He's anxious to hear more. Guess I will fill him in on the more, when I really know more."

"He must be a good friend to have. I think it's great that a straight couple cares about their friend, the gay guy. Just too many times the straights go their way and the gays go theirs. I'm glad you have them, as friends."

"Well, so do you now too. Well, you actually have not really met either one of them, but at least you have seen David."

"Yeah, and I know where David works, and if I want to find out any dirt about you, I know where I can go to find David. So just remember, friends are great, but then a guy can go to that friend and find out the real trash!"

"I swear, you are a mess man! Oh, well, that's okay." Cory stated as he grinned broadly at Jimmy. "We've not actually discussed anything about the real who we each are, like last names and all that shit, but last night I think I heard some stuff that tells me a lot about you."

With a very quizzed expression on his face, Jimmy asked, "Like what?"

"Well, the comment, 'the new family company man, the new Hallbrook guy just might be gay,' and then Clay wanted to do that pencil thing and he knew your Dad and the other big shots would be gone early. Well, I have to assume that your last name is Hallbrook, right?

"Yeah."

"And that since you just happen to be in construction, that perhaps you just might happen to be part of the Hallbrook Homes Construction Company family, right?"

"Sherlock, just where is your cape and hat? Yes, you are completely right! It was not intended to be any type of a secret. I'm sorry that we had not discussed it earlier so that you did not need to feel that you had to sort it out before I told you. Yeah, Grandpa is the original Hallbrook contractor. Dad and Bob and Dick are all part of the company. Dad is the Project Manager, so he is out in the field, Bob is like assistant to the company controller and Dick is, well I guess ahead of sales and marketing. His title is Sales Manager, but I think he is more like a VP for Marketing. Hey, no title, no pay! Right? Grandpa has never been known for passing out high titles. He knows high titles, get high paychecks."

"Well, what exactly is your title, or what are your responsibilities, then?"

"I'm a crew chief. After high school I got my BA in Business and then an MBA. After that, I worked in Southern California at a company that we have part ownership in. It's kind of a small construction company, but it keeps our licenses current and active there, and I worked over there for about a year and a half in the office, and then came back home. When they wanted me to come back home, I told 'em that I wanted to start on the job site just as if I was from the outside, and once I had worked on the job sites for a couple of years, then I would consider moving into something like an assistant project manager or into the real estate area. So that's me. I'm one of the guys out there climbing ladders, and one of the guys out there looking up as some other guy climbs the ladder above me. The company used to require that everybody had to wear long pants on the job. Last summer I finally got 'em to realize that almost all of the other construction companies let their workers wear shorts since they're cooler, and easier to move in, and so we changed our policy. Oh, I kind of forgot to tell them that climbing the ladders and watching the other guys climb the ladders might have been one of the reasons that I thought we should make the change."

"You said that your family knows you are gay, right?"

"Oh yeah! They've known for a long time. They've known since late high school. All the bosses of the company know. That is one of the real reasons that I am so surprised that Mark and Clay didn't know for sure. Damn, I've got to come up with something to get back at Clay with. I need to come up with something that is one-on-one, and something that I can keep up for awhile if things go right. Damn, I've got to come up with a goody!"

"Oh, okay. My last name is Hallbrook, and you know a lot about little ole me, now it's time for me to find out some about you. Do you come from some famous family with bad skeletons in your family closets? No, seriously. I find myself, already and totally, in love with a man that I have now known less than one day. I already consider him my soul mate, my lifetime partner, and I do not have any idea of what his last name is."

"Well – ready? This is really exciting! Walker! Cory Michael Walker! Nothing exciting, nothing famous, nothing wealthy, nothing but Walker!"

"Well, I certainly don't see any problem with that! Thank goodness it's not some funny long name that I cannot either remember, pronounce or spell! What type of work does your Dad do?"

"He's a CPA. He has his own business, and has two other CPA's that work for him. Nothing big like Hallbrook Homes. But hey, it has always put food on the table and a roof over our heads. I don't think it's ever been a Hallbrook roof, but none the less, a roof."

"Like I've always said, 'One roof's as good as another!' Well, no, come to think about it, I've never said that. And now that I stop and think about it, some roofs are not as good as others. If it leaks, it's not as good. Right?"

"Absolutely! Okay, Jimmy Hallbrook. Is Jimmy the real and formal name or is it a nickname?"

"No, Jimmy is the nickname. It's really James Daniel Hallbrook."

"I think I mentioned it once yesterday, but then didn't follow through with it. I do not like calling you 'Jimmy.' That's way too juvenile for a stud like you. I'm sorry but trying to call you 'Jimmy' is just way too – kiddish! If anybody ever asks me why I don't like calling you Jimmy, I'll just tell 'em – you let that guy stick that oversized big rod of his up in your ass and you'll decide pretty damn quickly that he does not need to be called any name that sounds like a young kid. There is no way to be a young kid and be hanging a dick like that! What else can I call you? Is Jim okay, or is there another nickname that you like?"

"You know Cory, I really don't have any idea of why I have always liked it, but ever since I have been a little kid, I've always wanted to be called 'Jimbo.' Don't ask me why. I have no idea, but I've always liked 'Jimbo.' What do you think about that?"

"Well, to be honest I like it better than Jimmy. Kind of different I admit, but hey, I have no problem of using something different for you. I consider you very different, why not a different name? When did you first decide you liked the name Jimbo?"

"The when, I'm not sure. I just know that when I was in grade school I decided I liked it. I don't know why!"

"Well, I have a theory," Cory interjected, "but of course, I don't know if I'm right or not. Was there anybody in your life back then that might have called you 'Jimbo' that you specifically liked? Did your father by any chance have any friends that might have called you Jimbo? I know it might sound weird, but as little kids, if we were paid some special attention by somebody that we really liked, that makes a very big impression on us. I just kind of wonder if some guy that you internally thought of as hot, might have called you Jimbo, and you have liked it ever since."

"Cory, I think you have hit on something! Yeah, when I was in about the fourth or fifth grade, we had a neighbor that I always thought a lot of. He was probably about college age, and I remember I always thought that he always looked and acted so nice. I suppose now that I've grown up and realized that I'm gay, I could assume I also liked the way he was built, but I just remember that I always liked to be around him. I always wanted to be close to him. I'm trying to remember what he called me. For some reason it seems like he called me, 'Hey you,' most of the time, but you know I do bet it was him! I was really hurt when he and his family moved away. Yeah, you know, I wanted to move with 'em. I felt all alone for awhile after they moved. You know what, I am starting to wonder if I was kind of in love with that guy, even though I was just a kid. You know Cory, even if it was not him that called me Jimbo at one time. I'm going to assume that it was! Yeah, call me Jimbo! I like that!"

"Done deal, man. Done deal! From this point in time on, if I ever happen to call you Jimmy, it's a total screw up. From now on, you are Jimbo. If anybody asks about it, let's just tell 'em that I didn't care for the Jimmy thing, and we decided to use Jimbo. We don't need to tell them about your early love, or whatever it was, okay?"

"Good, sounds like a plan to me! I guess the guys at work will still call me Jimmy, but maybe if we're around Mark and Keith very often, maybe Mark will start calling me Jimbo, and then maybe it'll get changed at the job."

"What about the family?"

"Hey, no problem there! They have been so anxious for me to find myself some great guy, that once I get a chance to tell 'em about you, I could tell 'em that you want me to run around naked all day, and they would think that is great! They've been so anxious to get a new son-in-law in the family, that whatever you want, it'll be great with them. I'll just tell them that you didn't want to call me Jimmy and we decided on Jimbo."

"Damn, I'm not attractive to you, just to please your family, am I? I mean, are you after me, or are you just filling a family responsibility? Hey, do remember, I'm not the type of person that can help you give 'em grandkids."

"No, no, not that problem! They just always tell me that they are tired of there being an odd number of people at the table, and that I need to find someone so that my partner would even out the number. Hey, the important things in life I guess!"

"Yeah, maybe so, but I sure am damn glad that they have that attitude, instead of thinking you should go find yourself some cute little lady all dressed up in her cute little pink dress!"

"Well, not you as much as me! I've always been so fortunate that my family has accepted me for who I am and has not been like so many families are when they find out about one of their kids. You know, Cory, I think you and I have been pretty damn fortunate. Stop and think about it, we both have pretty damn good families! Too many guys simply cannot say that! We need to be very thankful!"

"Okay man, enough family talk! We have all of the very formal stuff that needs to be arranged you know. Let's see – we'll need to rent a large hall, hire the catering company, find a florist, hire the limos, and make the proper setting to announce that you are now part of the Walker family and that I am now part of the Hallbrook family. I really do think this should be done in the Old English Style. All of the pomp and circumstance and all of that fancy stuff, now don't you? Oh yeah – also invite the Queen. I think that would be appropriate!"

"Hell no man! Just sent them an E-mail and tell them that they all have another person to buy Christmas presents for! Hey, let's go for the really important stuff. Like presents! Oh, yeah – if we had the big formal church wedding, two guys in tuxes, hey think of all of the toasters, electric skillets, irons and stuff we could get. Yeah, maybe we do need to do the big fancy, dancy thing!"

"Electric skillets? Do people still buy electric skillets? Hell, I have not heard anybody mention an electric skillet for years! Do they still sell those things? I guess I thought microwave ovens replaced them."

After finishing breakfast and picking up the dishes, and doing the other little clean-up stuff required to make a kitchen and dining area look presentable again, Cory and Jimbo, as he was now called, did decide to get dressed in some rather presentable but comfortable clothes and take the walk down by the lake that had been mentioned earlier.

"Hey, Jimbo, my man. What casual type of clothes did you bring over here for today? Let me see so that I can put on something similar, but not too much alike. I just want us to kind of look like we were planning on doing the same thing. I don't want it to look like one of us was planning on going fishing, and the other one thought we were going to a concert."

CHAPTER 2

The GMFPC Experience

After dressing, they started down the street and enjoyed the cool gentle morning air, and the aromas of the flower gardens that seemed to be so prevalent, in this particular neighborhood.

"This is a very well taken care of neighborhood, isn't it?" Jimbo commented. "Everybody certainly does seem to try and take care of their properties nicely, don't they?"

"Yeah – they do. There's quite a few older, retired, couples that live close to here. In fact, when I bought my place, I bought it from an elderly woman that was going into a senior living home. I really haven't seen too many younger people around here, but I think that as the older folks sell out and move on, then more of the younger set will start moving in. Everyone has always been very nice to me around here. I kind of think some of the older set is glad to see a younger person around once in awhile. I've had some of the old folks ask me how soon I was planning on getting married. Some said they really miss the little kids out and about playing, and riding their bikes and that type of stuff. Some of 'em have told me to hurry up and get married and have kids so they can watch the little ones grow up. And when I've told some of the more friendly ones not to expect that to happen, they just kind of frowned and said, 'Well, if that's the way it is, then that's the way it is.' One ole guy told me, 'Hey good! That means there's going to be two younger guys around here someday to help me take care of my place.' Then he said, 'That works for me!' I guess it sure didn't upset him too much!"

"You said you've been in this neighborhood for, what, two and a half years, right?"

"Yeah, I found my place shortly after getting introduced to the Calf's Skin, and that was when I started looking around here. My place has needed some fixing up, but that's okay, 'cause that meant I got to buy it a little cheaper, and I've been able to fix it up as I go – and as I can afford to."

"So does that mean that you've been pretty much of a stay at home type of guy the last few years, or have you had any chance to travel or go anyplace?"

"Well Jimbo, my man – you ought to know that I have not always been just a nice little stay at home type of a guy! Two years ago I had one damn good weekend, that I look back at very fondly. Have you ever heard of the event called the GMFPC?"

"No, sure haven't! What does that stand for, and what is that?"

"It stands for, Gay Men's Fucking Point Contest. It's an annual event held up by Denver, out in the country someplace, where gay guys compete to see who can pile up the most sex points, for about any and all, sexual activity accomplished that weekend."

"Sex points? How do you get sex points?"

"It's a four day get together where you get points for having all kinds of sex."

"Have you been to one of these – well, I guess maybe you have – right?" Jimbo questioned. "You went to one of these get-togethers?"

"Yeah, the one two years ago. I didn't get to go last year, but sure do wish I had!

"Where in the hell did you ever hear about something like this?"

"I heard about it in the bar one night. Of course, at that time I really knew nothing about it at all. Some guys were talking about it, but they were talking second hand. They hadn't been there either. The year before, a friend of theirs had been there and he's the one that had told 'em about it. I finally found a web site that referred to it, but very intentionally, it didn't give any real information. The web site didn't even explain what the initials stood for. There was a mailing address, if you wanted to request information, but no e-mail address or anything else. They were keeping this pretty close knit. They wanted to keep it so that just the guys that had happened to hear about it were the only ones asking for any info. I sent 'em a letter asking for more information about the annual 'party,' as I put it. I just wanted some kind of a reference in there, about the get together, so that they'd know that I did know something about it. I got a letter back explaining that it was a party by invite only. And the 'only' was capitalized."

"They were interested in seeing if I was an individual that should be considered for invitation, so they wanted some addition information about me. It was pretty detailed. All kinds of questions that you probably would not even ask some guy that you had just met at a bar. I guess they figured that if you were too timid to answer these questions then, you were too timid to be one of the guys for the party. They also said that, if I were going to be in the Denver area anytime soon, to please call a specific number to arrange a conversation with two of the hosts. If I was not going to be in the Denver area, then please do a five to ten minute video of myself explaining why I would like to attend and to mail it back to them. One strong requirement – you had to be nude! And, it had to show the face and the body! It didn't have to be anything sexual, but it did have to show the entire person. They were very specific in a statement, that those that could be personally interviewed, would be the top choice guys. There would be a total of only 41 guys. In other words, you and then 40 more guys to get points from."

"So what'd you do?"

"I went to Denver! I very neatly arranged a business requirement to visit one of the computer suppliers up there, and so I let the company send me to Denver for two days. I arranged it so that I would be there on company business Thursday and Friday, and then I'd return back here on Sunday afternoon. Worked out very nicely – if I do say so myself. When I called the number to tell 'em that I would be in Denver, the guy on the other end asked me when, and told me that somebody would call me back in fifteen minutes, and then he asked if I would be available to take the call? That was all that he said. I thought – Wow! Really quite mysterious! But right at fifteen minutes later, another guy called and told me to be standing on the southeast corner of Alameda and Downing Streets at 6:30 on that Friday evening. He told me to expect a green and white van to pull over with two guys in it. He said the one on the passenger side will ask me if I am Cory. They will then invite me to have dinner with them. I found out later that they quickly decide, between themselves, if it is going to be dinner at McDonald's or a nice sit down dinner someplace. From what I was told, if you knew the scheme ahead of time, and you ended up at a McDonald's, then you might just as well excuse yourself, because you had already been rejected. Fortunately, they took me to a very nice steak house. Someplace I guess they go to quite often, since the girl at the front desk called 'em by name. They asked for a specific waiter and I did notice that when he approached the table, he eyeballed me up one side and down the other. He made a comment, that at the time I didn't quite understand. He said, 'You gentlemen will certainly have a very good dinner this evening, I see.' I found out later that what he was referring to was – me! He was part of the whole thing. He was giving them his approval from what he could see. He was part of the organization planning committee."

"After we had dinner, all paid for by them, which I thought was rather nice since I do know that was no five dollar dinner, they then suggested, but in a rather, 'we will do' attitude, go to Jim's apartment. I said okay! I figured I'm in town till Sunday afternoon anyway, so off we went. On the way, and soon after we got there, we just had small talk about Denver, and the computer business, since they knew that was what I did, and then things really kind of got down to the true 'why' we were there. They reminded me that although we certainly were enjoying each others company, I was there to be interviewed, and to please take everything off. Well, I do have to admit that I have never been in somebody's living room, on the 18th floor of an apartment building, standing in front of a floor to ceiling window with the drapes completely open, and then get totally nude! They saw me glance toward the window, and asked me it that created a problem for me. I quickly said, 'No,' and then I took everything off! I, in-fact, had my ass toward the window when I bent over to take off my briefs. I thought, okay guys, I'll show you and anybody looking in from the other buildings that I do have an ass, and if you would like to see it, here it is! I figured, hey, it's not my apartment and if anybody sees anything, they don't know who I am anyway! Right? Well, I guess maybe I didn't react quite as timidly as they expected me to. Putting my ass, kind of up in the air like that, and not being afraid of who might see it was, I guess, maybe a little more than they expected. One of 'em, and I really don't know for sure which one, told the other one, 'Hey man, I think maybe we have a real participant here, and maybe we had better close those drapes! They closed the drapes. I gathered that they usually did that with some guy, so that they could find out just how brazen that guy was, and usually the guy never shows everything like I did! They did make a comment about me not being timid in front of others. I felt like – hey, maybe I'm making points here! And I guess I was! I was then taken by the hand and led into the bedroom. Well, from that point in time on, I guess all I can say is that I was auditioned in all of the possible rolls that I might be expected to perform – if I were to get an invite! I've heard of 'the casting couch' in the movies industry – well, let me tell you that no couch would have worked for this interview! I don't know if these two guys "work together" all of the time or not, but they certainly did make a great team checking me out! I really don't think I failed at any activity that they got me involved in, and they got me involved in everything imaginable! Chains, ropes, candle wax, tit clamps – you name it – I was definitely checked out! At that time – hey – get an invite or not, I sure had one hell of a good evening playing with two hot guys, and besides, they bought me a nice dinner too! I thought, what a great way to get to ask for a party invitation. I decided the asking part, was just as good as the party. After they 'allowed' me to shower, they then told me that although they could not make the official invite, that it has to come in the mail, to make damn sure I kept the Thursday, Friday, Saturday and Sunday of the get-together open. They already knew that I would be very busy that particular weekend. That night at the apartment, we got involved in more stuff than what went on at the get-together. I think they had just found themselves a very active playmate, and used me to their advantage. And I didn't bitch about it at all! Believe me, not at all!

They filled me in a little more on the scoring system. They told me that since they already knew I'd be there, that it was okay to give me some of the finer points of the get together. They suggested that if I really wanted to rack up some major points, to get myself one of the really big dildos. Maybe like the one that is about nine inches around at the head and has about a twelve or thirteen inch shaft. Learn to use that as easily as possible, or at least, get used to feeling something like that, when it goes in, and then I'll be able to take about anything there, and will really rack up the points! I know you haven't seen it yet, but that's why I have the big dildo, that I call 'Big Bill.' Bill is the fake name that I was assigned when my invite arrived, and since I had bought that dildo to get ready for that weekend, that's why I call it, 'Big Bill.'

"So what happened then? Like how did you know where to go and that kind of stuff?"

"If and when you got an invite, you were given instructions to go to a certain bath house, there in Denver at a certain time, very early, like 2 AM on that Thursday, and tell the guy at the window that you're part of the contest. He then lets you in, gives you a locker number and tells you to go put everything in the locker, except the gym shorts and shirt you were told to bring, and any necessary personal stuff like medicine, glasses, toothbrush or other stuff that you need to take with you for the weekend. We weren't allowed to bring anything else. No poppers, nor medicine – that wasn't a prescription medicine, with your name on it. No other clothes. Only the shorts you were told to wear, and of course a shirt and shoes. No cell phones! We were told that, in the invitation letter – like about three times! We were told to put everything else in the locker and to lock it with the lock that we were told to bring. After we did that, then we were to go into the TV room and wait until everybody else got there. They had food in there for us, so the wait, which took about an hour, wasn't too bad. It also gave us a chance to start meeting each other. Hey, the idea was, if we were going to be fucking each other all weekend, then we might just as well start meeting each other, right away!"

"After everybody got there, they loaded us up on two busses and headed out. Where we went – I have no idea! The drive took us about an hour, and with the lights on inside of the bus, and the window shades pulled down, we really couldn't see out of the windows. The bus drivers were definitely part of this group! They were not just hired drivers. There is no way some hired driver is going to be part of this group!"

"While we were still on the bus, everybody was issued their score cards that we kept and that we added our points up on. One was called the PAC card which stood for Personal Achievements Card and the other was the

Activities Card. Points were awarded for even being nude on the bus. I think that was to start getting us in the mood, and to see how many guys really had the guts to be out on a bus, totally nude. I have to admit that at first I might have been kind of hesitant, but then when the bus driver pulled over and got himself totally undressed, I figured – if he can – then so can I! When he did that, I was wanting to go up front and help him drive. He was a hot fucking driver! Well, his driving might not been so hot, but damn he carried one hell of a hot body!"

"We came to some really very nice resort type of a place, really back, some back roads, so it was very private. I rather liked the way we were greeted by the all male staff. As the busses drove up to the front of the entrance, all of 'em, and I'd say probably about twenty five of them, came out, and all lined up, as if for inspection, dressed only in their black leather jock straps! Very, very nice presentation, if I may say so! And this was now like at about four or four thirty in the morning! Some of those guys, I am sure, would have rather been in bed. But they were all there and looking very sharp! Although – with them – the points did not count! I'm sure they made some points with some of the guys that weekend anyway! Damn, the whole group of 'em was hot!"

"They had pretty well informed us of all of the things that we needed to know while we were still on the bus. We kind of went over the contest rules again, just to make sure that everybody understood, and to see if there were any questions."

"Each time you got fucked, fucked somebody else, got fisted or fisted somebody else, you got points. You got extra points for getting double fisted. Shit man! I bet that if you had been there, any guy that got fucked by you, could have gotten extra points for just showing that he could get that damn big dick of yours, up in himself!"

"Yeah – right," Jimmy grinned, responded, and laughed back.

"They had a collection of different size dildos that, when you took one up your ass, you got points. The number of points depended on the size of the dildo. That big one is why I thought about you. Damn near just about the same size as your dick!"

"Every time one of the dildos was used, it was completely cleaned and sterilized, and then waiting on the next guy. That was one of the responsibilities of the young guys that wore the small tight little black leather jock straps all weekend. Keeping everything nice and clean and tidy for everybody all weekend."

"We had about six guys, out of our whole group, that rotated as the scorekeepers. Whenever they were acting as a scorekeeper, they wore bright red trunks so that everybody knew that they were – at that time – a scorekeeper. While they were a scorekeeper, they couldn't participate. In other words, if they fucked a guy while they were acting as a scorekeeper, those points didn't count. Points didn't count for them, and didn't count for you either! So if you wanted to fuck around with one of the guys in the red shorts, it was because you were either just so damn hot for him, or him for you, that the idea of the contest was of no importance right then! His ass, or your ass, was the really important thing right then!"

"You could either get a scorekeeper to document your points, or if you needed to, if no scorekeeper happened to be available right then, three other guys could document it for you. If a scorekeeper happened to be around, it was usually easier to just have him do it. Whatever was happening meant that two guys were getting points, one the giver, and the other one, the receiver – so two cards always had to be marked. You could fuck around with anybody, whenever you wanted to, but if you wanted that fucking to count, then you had to get a scorekeeper to come score it on your card or have three guys document it. Oh, and yeah, you got extra points for multiple actions all at once! Like, if your hands were chained down – that was two points. If your ankles were chained down that was two points, but if both your hands and your feet were chained at the same time, then you got an extra two points on top of the other four. So if your hands, and your feet were chained, you were gagged, you were blindfolded, and you were getting fisted, that totaled up to something like about twenty points for just that one session. If you were tied down, then you had to rely on one of your buddies to get the scorekeeper to give you your points. But there was never any problem there. Everybody was always trying to help the other guys add up their points. I think that's the whole purpose of the entire weekend! It's to see how much sex they can have, and then prove they've had it! Let's see! Fucking was two points, getting fucked was four points, having your hands tied – two points, feet tied – two points, gagged – two points, blindfolded

– two points, getting fisted – four points, doing some fisting – two points, getting double fisted by one guy, that was six points, but getting double fisted by two guys, that was, I think, ten points. A hand and a dildo up in your ass all at once was four points for the hand plus the points for the dildo, depending on its size, plus extra points for the double action! Oh yeah! Butt plugs! They had a big variety of different sizes, and the biggest one gave you something like twenty points. That damn thing was a real ass stretcher. It hurt my ass just to look at it and even think about it going up in my ass. I really don't know if anybody there, that entire weekend, ever took that dildo. I saw a lot of guys trying to, or at least playing with it. I'm sure it was something bigger than they had ever tried to push up in their asses before. I know one guy played with it for well over an hour. Some of us thought he ought to get points for just trying so long and so hard. But he didn't! Wasn't on the list of things you could get points for!"

"Oh, if you got double fucked by two guys, that was something like about twelve points. They had the pointing system arranged so that doing the double stuff and having more than one man on you or in you at the same time really added up the points! Oh! Yeah – your PAC card! Your PAC card had each guy's fake name on it. Beside the name was a place for him to initial it. He put his initials on it if he had fucked you, gotten fucked by you, fisted you, or been fisted by you! For each check mark or initial, you got two points. But for each guy, where all of his four places were marked, you then got an extra six points. So if you did all four with that guy, then you totaled fourteen points – just on that one card – for that one guy, regardless of what else had happened. The scoring on that card, which they called your PAC card, which stood for 'Personal Achievements Card,' was different points than the, 'Activities Card.' So fuck a guy, get the fucking points on the Activities Card, and if this is the first time you have played with this guy, you get the points on the Personal Achievements Card too. It figured out that if you just did the stuff listed on your PAC card, and did it with all forty other guys, then you would automatically have 960 points without getting points for doing anything like gagging, blindfolded or anything like doubling. I think the guy that got the most points on his PAC card had played with thirty two of the guys in some one fashion or another. The weekend I was there, there wasn't anybody that had played with, or gotten points for playing with all forty guys. The guy that got the most points on his PAC card and the one that had the most 'over all' points, got a free invite back, the next year. So two guys got a free visit the next year."

"The cost was $350 which, at first, I thought was pretty steep, but once I got there and saw what the place was like, and what the food was, it was damn well worth it! Besides, they supplied all of the linens, poppers, grease, clamps, chains, candles, rubbers, gags, blindfolds and everything else we needed! Actually the $350 was probably less than what they could have gotten from the normal regular guests. This place must be owned by some gay guys, 'cause, to close up the resort for all other business for the weekend to do this? They had to have some damn good reason to do this each year! And they must have hired special workers for this weekend, too! Well hell! I guess they would have had too, unless they already had that many hunky, good looking, gay guys on staff that they could use."

"And oh, shit! The dinners that they had were great! Especially the desserts! The desserts were always something in the shape of a dick and balls. One night they had cakes that I swear, I thought at first, were actual dildos! Pancakes in the morning were in the shape of dicks, instead of round. And of course you can imagine they used bananas for everything imaginable! All the waiters wore their very classy black jock straps. They had a "law" that you could touch one of the servers only – if the server, or worker, whatever they were called, did ask to be touched. You could indicate that you really wanted to rub him, but it was up to him to say yes, or indicate to you, not to. They were very, very playful, so they accepted your approach almost all of the time! About the only time when they didn't, was when they had something hot in their hands, or had to really take care of something important. They had free rein of touching the contestants whenever they wanted to though! You could be sitting there, maybe at the dining table, feel something on the side of your face, turn and find out that one of them had his crotch right at your mouth level. We finally figured out that they were all trying to see how many guys they could each find, where a guy's face and his own crotch just happened to be at the same level when he walked up to him. This was a bad thing for the really tall guys. They kind of got left out on this since they were always too high for the guys to walk up to and have their crotch at the right height."

"We found out that part of the time, before the workers came into the main rooms, where we were at, they would kind of jerk off, out in the hallway, getting himself kind of hard, because each of 'em was always trying to make his dick, in his jock strap, always look bigger than the other guys.' For a joke one night, one of 'em, one of the workers, stuck a baked potato in his jock strap and then paraded around. Gawd man! Some of the guys there got really excited, until they found out it was a potato. Shit man! It's too damn bad you weren't there! You wouldn't have needed the potato! With that dick of yours, your jock strap would have stuck out just as far as his did!"

"If you wanted to, you could wear your shorts to the dining room to eat, but if you did, they deducted five points off of your total points, for each time you wore the shorts. Nobody wore anything to eat in! You could lay your napkin on your leg, but – if somebody caught you laying it across your dick and kind of hiding it, they were then allowed to stand up and yell out, 'We've got a 'hider' in the house,' and then point at the poor guy. After the first time of that, everybody made damn sure he wasn't hiding his dick. The 'hider,' then had to deduct one point from his card. There was a place where you had to list your 'deduct' points so that when they added the totals up, they could deduct whatever you had to deduct. Oh, on the point system – I forgot about the sucking and getting sucked. I think, if I remember right, the sucking got four points and the getting sucked got two points."

"Like, how many points did you get, do you remember?"

"Oh yeah! I got a total of 634 points total for the weekend. I still have my official points earned, certificate!"

"What? You actually got a certificate for your points?"

"Yeah, it's called the 'The Official Certificate of Fucking Points Earned During one Fucking Good Time,' and then the dates, and it says, 'Presented by: GMFPC.' Oh it looks really, really, very official! I think the guy that got the most points on both his Activities Card and his Personal Achievements Card was something like about 850 points. I've gotta admit though, I've just never quite found the right wall, where I can hang up my certificate. I really don't think that's a certificate that I can group with my other company certificates on my office wall. Do you?"

CHAPTER 3

My Saturday Friend

"I gotta admit I don't think it was as exciting as your weekend, but yes, I did have one day not too long ago that really did go kinda on the weird and different side.

"While I was living in Southern California for a while, one day I was driving around town on a Saturday morning, through the parks, down the kind of back allies, of the somewhat sleazier parts of town, and checking out the guys at every bus stop that I happened to drive past – and that drive was simply my 'inner proof,' that I really needed to find himself, either, number one, a life-partner, or number two, at least some guy that I could depend on having a good sex session with at least once in awhile."

"Friday night had not exactly been one of my most successful times in finding some good, hot, active sex action. And my Saturday morning search for – that missing action – was not turning out to be a very good recovery program."

"Friday night had turned out to be one of those, 'go home alone, jerk off in bed, go to sleep,' and wake up Saturday morning still 'horny as hell,' occasions!"

"After fixing some breakfast and reading the Saturday morning newspaper, I simply could not get my mind off of the fact that I really wanted, and I really needed some sex."

"My Saturday morning, 10AM drive around town looking for a guy to play with certainly was not my idea of how to live my life, but that is actually what was happening. I had been through all of the 'more probable' areas of town, places where I thought perhaps other very horny guys just might be hanging out at, but it looked like that day, I was the only gay guy in town that had gone 'without,' the night before."

"After driving around for about an hour or a little longer, and having no hint of any possible success, I was just about ready to give it up and just have to live with the idea of being good and horny until I could either give himself enough exciting sex, or finally find some guy with a big and willing dick to take care of me."

"The unexpected sight of Mary's Breakfast Cafe made up my mind for me immediately. I did not realize exactly where I was, but this cafe was a very welcome sight. I had eaten there just after I had gotten to town, and I remembered the food was really outstanding."

"Hell, no sex! I thought I might as well have good food!"

"Mary's Breakfast Cafe did serve food all day, but because of its outstanding reputation for its breakfast meals, I was told the name had been changed a few years ago to include the word 'Breakfast.' The cafe was a small stand-alone building, with cute little flower boxes hanging from the windows. The building really kind of made you feel like you were in somebody's house."

"I parked my car, and after entering and looking around for an empty space, I found himself a seat at the counter. As I sat down, I turned to the young gentleman seated beside me, and remarked, 'Busy place isn't it?'"

"The gentleman turned toward me and replied, 'Yeah, it sure is! I don't get in here very often, especially this time of day, and I had to wait for a seat before I could even sit down. They sure do, do the business. Do you eat here often?'"

"I told him, 'No, I just happened to be in the area, and I ate here some time ago and I remembered how good their breakfast was, so I made a last minute decision to stop in. I already had one breakfast this morning, but I guess I'll have a second one.'"

"As I removed the menu from its holder and started checking it out, the man beside me then remarked, 'Second breakfast of the day? You didn't know you were going to be coming in here then I assume, right?'"

"As I continued to browse the menu, I said, 'No, I didn't. Kind of a confusing morning for me, I guess. I was just out riding around and ended up here. Didn't know where I was headed when I left the house.'"

"The waitress gave me a glass of water and asked if I was ready to order. I told her, 'Yeah. I'll have the two eggs, over well done, and wheat toast. No meat. Black coffee, and a small orange juice, please.'"

"I put the menu into its holder and the man beside me extended his hand and said, 'Good morning. I'm Nick.'"

"I did likewise and replied, 'Oh, thanks, I'm Jim.'"

"Then he asked, 'So I rather guess you are not from this area, right? I mean if it has been sometime since you have been in here, I guess you are kind of a visitor in the area. Right?'"

"I told him, 'Yeah, right. I live up on the northeast corner of town, and I just happened to be out on an aimless drive this morning, and I recognized the place, so I just decided to stop in and eat again.'"

"He said, 'Well good. I mean – good you stopped in. Aimless drive, uh? Kind of sounds like you are a little unorganized today then, right?'"

"I then turned, and as I looked the guy over just slightly, I said, 'Yeah, just kind of feeling all alone and was out looking to see if anything exciting was happening in town this week-end, that I should know about.'"

"As I replied, and took a little more of an interest in the young man and his attempted conversation, I thought, 'Certainly interested in what and why I'm doing what I'm doing, but not a bad looking guy at all! I thought, hey Jimbo, talk to the man! Be friendly! Might pay off.'"

"He said, 'Yeah, know what you mean. I'm kind of somewhat in the same situation today. My wife and the kids are at a church camp this week-end up at the lake, and so I'm trying to be the 'home-alone-daddy.' That's why I'm in here eating. The cold cereal at home certainly was not exciting to me.'"

"I turned to him and asked, 'So your wife and the kids are camping, but you didn't go?'"

"He said, 'Yeah, the kids are only three and five years old, and if you send any kids that are under the age of eight, then a parent has to be involved, and go too, so I shipped Jane and the kids off yesterday, and they get back Monday afternoon. I couldn't go. I've got stuff that needs to be done here, and besides, this will give her a little extra time with the kids all by herself.'"

"I told him, 'Oh, okay,' as I took my breakfast plate from the waitress and started eating. The conversation from this point was rather hit and miss, but I did keep it going. My thought was, 'Oh, nice looking daddy, about maybe twenty-five or twenty-six years old, looks like he might workout some, home alone until Monday afternoon, is friendly to me, he started the conversation, must live someplace close by here. Mommy and the kiddies are gone out of town – wonder why I happen to already know that? I continued the conversation, and tried to keep it very friendly."

"He asked me some rather interesting questions such as, what type of work do I do, where did I grow up, was I still single. Items that in any other situation, might not have been noticeable, but to me, on that day, each of his questions just happened to be the type that guys will ask other guys, if they are looking for something – something that they cannot come right out and ask for. But then, I thought, I'm horny, I know I'm horny and maybe I am really over reacting to some guy that is just being friendly."

"In extending the conversation, I did find out that Nick lived in the neighborhood, worked out of his home office, had only lived in town about two years, did go to the local gym a couple of times a week, and certainly did not know how to cook."

"Keeping my ears open for any possible opportunity to take this conversation to 'the next level,' if that is where it might be going to, I said to him, 'Hey Nick – want some more coffee or something? I'm enjoying our conversation, and since I really don't have a damn thing that I need to get done today, I am really enjoying our talking together.'"

"He did motion to the waitress that he could use some more coffee, and then told me, 'Yeah, I am too. Being home all alone, I'm not used to that! Gets very lonesome. Hey, you just said that you don't have anything important to do today – would you be interested in maybe coming over to my place and watching the football game on TV with me? One look at you and I can tell you are definitely the kind of a guy that is into sports, right?'" I told him, 'Yeah Nick, if it's okay with you, I definitely would like to kick back and watch the game with someone that understands football. I like to make comments when some stupid play is done or some bad official call is made, but usually I am the only one in the room to make a comment back. Yeah Nick, I think that would be fun, if it's okay with you!'

He said, 'It's fine with me. I'm going to go crazy being all by myself this week-end. I sure could use some company in the house for awhile.'

"We left the cafe, and he told me to follow him, that the house was only a couple of blocks away."

"As I got into my car, I decided that I needed to calm myself down some. Nothing, absolutely nothing, had been said or implied that this was to be anything other than watching a football game on TV with a lonesome, married, guy. A guy that is a very nice person to talk to, and maybe, just perhaps, a man that would like to have somebody in the house for awhile. I thought, 'Just because I'm gay and horny – and he is hot and built – that does not mean that anything is intended, other than watching the game together.'"

"As we got to the house, I parked my car and followed him in the side door. He asked me, 'Hey, do you want some coke or 7-up or maybe some more coffee? I don't drink beer, so I don't have any to offer you, but if you want something else, you sure are welcome to it.'"

"I told him, 'No, not right now! Maybe later. Right now I'm too full from having the two breakfasts.'"

"Then he told me, 'Okay. Hey Jim, I'll be right back. I had a meeting this morning and that's why I've got these dress clothes on, and your shorts and T-shirt looks much more comfortable to me, so I'm going to go change, I'll be right back.'"

"He headed for the bedroom area, and I found himself a comfortable place on the couch, and started flipping TV channels to find the game."

"As he came into the living room, I actually hoped that my jaw did not drop as I took the first glimpse of him in his shorts and his T-shirt! He had a very hot, and a very attractive athletic body, and he definitely knew how to wear clothes that showed it off. I attempted to 'regroup' himself from the beautiful shock that I had just undergone, and I hoped that he hadn't noticed my reaction."

"When he came in and asked if the game was on yet, I told him, 'Yeah, well anyway the pre-game show is on. I guess the game must start in a little while.'"

"Before he sat down, he closed some drapes on the front window and said, 'That much light coming in makes the TV hard to see.'"

"I just said, 'Oh, okay.' But then I thought, 'Too much light? It's not really that bright! Hmmmmm?' Then I wondered if he wanted a little more privacy in there? I thought, 'Oh God, I hope so! Damn tight, short shorts!' I gotta tell you, I thought those were a little too tight to usually be worn at the gym!"

"I watched him as he closed the drapes. His ass was right there in front of me, and I know damn well my tongue was getting wet just wanting to step over there and run it up and down that tight looking ass! And then he turned around and started back across the room. I thought, 'Oh shit man! Oh man, is that basket all him, or am I just imagining stuff again only because I'm horny?' I thought maybe I had better get out of there before I did something stupid and assumed this was something different than what it really was. I do mean, straight guys do have good bodies, and straight guys do have big baskets if they happen to have big dicks, and some of 'em like to show their stuff off, but that don't mean they're gay. I kept telling myself to, 'Calm down! He's a married, straight daddy.' Then I thought, 'Oh shit, I shouldn't tell myself that!' That was just making me that much more horny!"

"All of sudden he said, 'I personally think these pre-game shows are a waste of time. It's the ball game I'm interested in, not these former players that needed a job, so the networks came up with this idea of an hour of pre-game show, just to give 'em something to do. Let's get the game going, I want to see the Redskin's new uniforms.'"

"'Whoa,' I thought to myself. 'He wants to see the new uniforms? Hey the only reason to look at the uniforms is to imagine the body that is tucked inside of them.'"

"I told him, 'Yeah, I heard they are supposed to have new uniforms on today. I sure would like to know what kind of material they use to make 'em with. That has got to be some damn strong material.'"

"He looked at me and said, 'Yeah. I know! The way those guys tear around out there, it sure seems that the way they throw each other around, some of those jerseys should rip right off of them, doesn't it?'"

"I told him, 'Uh yeah!' But I really hesitated saying it. I was seriously wondering just where this conversation was headed."

"Then he told me that when he was in college, his part time work was working in the athletic department laundry room, and he often looked to see if he could find some label that said what type of material it was, but he never found one. Then he told me, 'Let me tell you, those guys must really stink when they get out of those uniforms. Their uniforms really reek with sweat. There was one guy that worked with 'em that really didn't mind the stench. When they had some that were almost too over done on stink, they'd let him do 'em. He always said it never bothered him, so they always sorted out the really strong stuff for him. He said he didn't know if he couldn't smell anything, or if they really didn't bother him any.'"

"I thought, 'Wow! Really into the stinking football jerseys, thing. That's something most guys would never mention – unless there was a real reason!'"

"As he was talking, I picked up a magazine and attempted to appear as if I was looking at it, but it was actually to cover the hard-on that I had growing, kinda due to the rather complete description of how stinky the football uniforms had been. I really wondered if he was aware of how he was talking and what he was talking about! Did he intend to talk this way, or was he simply making innocent conversation?"

"As he crossed the room, telling me about his college laundry experiences, he tucked his T-shirt into his shorts and knowingly or unknowingly, he appeared to almost be doing a sexy dance in front of me. The small twist to the left, to tuck in on the right, then the small twist to the right to tuck in on the left, then of course the hand down the front to tuck in the front, and I was really starting to wonder just how much of this was I going to be able to take, or was I going to be able to keep myself under control."

"I watched him and thought, 'Jimmy, if you don't calm yourself down, you could have trouble here. He is simply a straight man that has got you all turned on! Stay calm, cool and collected, man!'"

"He came across the room and sat down on the other end of the couch. I was almost relieved that he sat down over there, rather than in front of me. This way I'd be able to keep my eyes on the TV, and not on the crotch of death, that I was wanting to grab ahold of, so very, very badly right then!"

"I remained a little on the silent side for a few minutes, just in an attempt to see what was going to be happening next, and then he positioned himself so that he was rather reclining back, and he had put his feet up on the coffee table in front of him. He was bare footed. When he changed clothes, he didn't put any shoes or socks back on. Even the sight of his bare feet was a beautiful sight to me. As I sat there and tried to keep my eyes elsewhere, I realized that this was the very first time that a man's bare feet were turning me on. Never before had I ever wanted to suck on a man's toes before. Oh, that day I did! The idea was really getting me all hot and bothered! I knew I was really starting to kind of lose my self-control. I straightened myself up, I took a couple of deep breaths and attempted to get my mind on something else by telling him, 'You have a very pretty home here. I like it!'"

"He told me, 'Oh thanks, man. I give Jane the credit for the interior decorating. I take no credit there. She's the one with talent around here for doing that kind of stuff.'"

"'Oh yeah, Jane,' I thought. 'I'm glad he mentioned her again, just so that I didn't forget – he is married. Not gay – just married and a nice guy! Not gay!' I knew I had to remember that!"

"The football game got started and the conversation turned primarily to that. Once the new uniforms were available, that did create some concern for me since I was forced to refrain from my much desired comments about how damn tight those uniform pants were and how I wanted, so very badly, to go pull on the crotch of most of them, just to give 'em a little more room for their 'private' parts. I wanted to tell him that I was just simply sure their nuts had to hurt being pulled up that tight."

"Then I wondered if maybe I was then acting a little too stand-offish, and perhaps not acting enough like guys usually do. I was so damn afraid that I was gonna lose my sexual self-control, and that I had not been making any of the normal male comments that would usually be expressed between two completely comfortable guys."

"As we commented on the new uniforms, I did decide that I needed to make at least one side comment that sounded rather 'manly' so that Nick didn't wonder why I acted so damn – kid like. So I told him, 'Well, Nick, I don't know either, what material they use, but all I can say right now is that I'm damn glad it's not my nuts that are squeezed up in there like theirs are. Maybe that's the reason they get paid so much money to play a game. Hurt my nuts, pay my bucks!'"

"He looked at me and said, 'Hey, I like that! Hurt my nuts, pay my bucks!' Hey that is cute! I got to see if I can remember that one!'"

"I felt a little more calmed then. I thought maybe he'd now just take me as a good guy, and not wonder why I was acting so up-tight."

"I noticed that as the game progressed, he got more and more relaxed on the couch and continued to recline more and more. A couple of times, he'd make a comment about how his back was bothering him, and his usual hot morning shower hadn't made it feel better that day, like it normally does."

"I was still having my own personal problems, but they certainly were not pain problems. They were control problems. His very short and very tight shorts, the big basket inside of those shorts, the bare feet, the tight T-shirt and the athletic body were all grouping to create some major problems for me. He was fucking hot, and I do mean hot! After all, I had been out driving around looking for something hot since I was horny as hell, and here this straight guy was, right beside me!"

"The ball game was not going well. It was a completely one sided game. Both of us agreed that that game was not turning out to be very exciting."

"Then after we decided that the game was no good, he said, 'Hey, my back is really bothering me. It's what they always refer to as an old football injury! Well, actually mine is kind of football related, but in a different way. As a little kid I was pushed off of the bleachers on the sidelines of a football field, and I spent a few days in the hospital and have had back problems ever since. Real football injury – right! Anyway, the hot shower usually helps it, but today I'm not wearing my back support, and so now it hurts. Have you ever given anybody a body massage, before?'"

"Very hesitantly but yet firmly, I answered, 'Yeah, do you want me to see if I can help it any for you?'"

"He told me, 'Hey Jim, if you would, I'd really appreciate it. Jane will usually rub it out for me, but of course you know that's not possible today. Let me get a big towel and some skin cream and I'll lie down here on the floor, if that's okay with you.'"

"I told him, 'Yeah, that's fine with me.'"

"He returned with a big beach towel for on the floor, some skin cream and a smaller towel for me to use if I needed it."

"After he laid the towels down he told me, 'I'm gonna turn this TV off, if you don't mind. I've had enough of this game – if that's what you want to call it – and just having it nice and quiet in here while you rub my back, I think would be great.'"

"I told him, 'Yeah, fine with me. Yeah – that was one pathetic game today anyway! I'm sure the TV networks are always pissed when that happens. Just like us, – we quit watching it before they got all of their commercials aired.'"

"After he turned the TV off, he removed his T-shirt and laid down. I kneeled down beside him, and after putting some cream on my hands and some on his back, I started his massage."

"I had been around athletes, and of course gays, long enough to have plenty of massage experience. I was working his back and shoulders very well. The sighs and the moans coming from him were a good indication of that. As I moved his massage down toward his waist line, he did reach back and attempt to lower his shorts some, so that I could do his waist completely. His shorts were very, very tight on his body, and they simply would not lower down very easily. I attempted to massage his lower back, but my hands kept running into his shorts."

"I rather hesitantly asked, 'Uhh, hey, Nick. Would it be okay if we slid your shorts off while I do your lower back? They're in the way, and I can't get you rubbed down the way you should be. I can't get your lower back.'"

"'Uh, okay,'" he said. He raised his body up enough to pull the shorts off, and I was really surprised to see that Nick did not have a jock strap or any briefs on under those shorts."

"I went back to massaging his lower back. I was treating him to a very good, and a very through treatment. As I worked on his back, I absolutely could not keep my eyes off of that tight bubble butt that was now right in front of me. My hands kept getting closer and closer to his butt cheeks. He didn't complain any. I know he knew where my hands were at, and he never said anything. He just laid there and let me do my thing."

"I finally decided that if I was doing wrong, he'd let me know. I let both hands continue sliding down, and I slid a hand across each butt cheek. Nick moaned, but it was a good moan, and he never said anything about not touching that area. I started pulling my hands back up – once again massaging his muscular, round, and firm, butt cheeks. As I watched the action that I was doing on his rear end, I couldn't help from thinking, 'Oh man! What a pretty, pretty bubble butt!' And it was man, it was! It was one hot ass!"

"He let out a low moan, and said, 'Oh Jimmy, that feels so good. Please do that again!'"

"And I did! I did what he wanted! I continued massaging his butt cheeks and realized that if he was straight or gay, right now it did not matter. He was getting a very enjoyable treatment, and I was truly enjoying giving that treatment to him! I sure as the hell was not gonna stop!"

"I continued the butt massage. Then I grabbed some more skin cream and put it between his butt cheeks. Then I paused to see what reaction I'd be getting. I got no reaction! He continued to calmly just lie there and accept what was happening back there."

"I slide my right hand down between his butt cheeks. He spread his legs slightly as if to give me an, 'Okay – you're doing good,' signal."

"He slightly moaned and very quietly told me that everything was feeling better than any massage he had ever received. He told me, 'Jim, I have never been treated this lovingly before! Jim this is great! This is unbelievable! I never expected this to ever happen to me. This is great!'"

"As he was complementing me for the great feelings that he was being given, he very, very quickly, and all if a sudden, rolled over onto his back!"

"All of a sudden he said, 'Oh Jimmy, oh man! Oh Jimmy, I have never, ever asked a guy to do this before, but oh Jimmy, can you suck on my dick for me please? Oh, I've never done this before, but oh please, could you please?'"

"When he rolled over, he was supporting an enormous hard-on! When he rolled over it stood straight up in the air. I know his excitement was making his dick harder than it had probably ever been before. And I know he knew that!"

"He looked at me and told me, 'Oh Jimmy, I have never played with another guy before. No other guy has ever touched my dick before, but oh, right now I do want you to suck on it – if you would please man! He said, 'Oh Jimmy I hope you will suck on my dick. Please tell me that you do, and that you'll suck on me man!'"

"I was kind of sitting there in a complete shock, and at the same time, in complete pleasure of looking at that stiff eight inch dick that was begging for a mouth. My mouth!"

"I told him, 'Yeah Nick, I do suck dick – but you're a married man, with kids. Are you real sure you want this? Are you real sure that you won't regret it later? Am I so obviously gay looking, that you knew just by looking at me, that I would probably be a good one to get on your dick?'"

"He told me, 'No, no! Jimmy, I did not even think of you as being gay or being a guy that might suck on my dick until you put your hand up in my ass. When you started doing that to me, you just got me so damn hot and turned on! Nobody has ever been that loving to me. When you did that, I just prayed that we could do more! Jimmy I have never felt like this with any other person! Yeah, even my wife! She has never put her hand up in there. She has never even tried to rub my ass like that! Nobody has ever touched my ass like that! Oh what you have done for me today is so great! I will remember this forever.' And then he again asked, 'Oh, please, can you suck on my dick, please? Jimmy, if you can, please, I want to always remember that you cared enough for me on this day, that you let me put my dick in your mouth. Right now, it's more – more so that I can always remember how great this day has been, for me! I want to be able to remember that you took all of me, today. Jimmy, I want you to suck on my dick, please! Would you please?' Then he told me that before just a few minutes ago, he had never even thought about being with another guy, but right then, he wanted me to suck on him."

"Without saying anything, I grabbed his big rod, and slowly and lovingly placed it in my mouth. I heard him moan in pleasure! I slowly moved my mouth down along the long shaft of his dick. I sucked and sucked! After reaching the bottom of his shaft, I pulled back and once again sucked on his cock head, just like I had done earlier. I then, again, lowered my mouth down along the shaft and licked the sides of his dick as I went down. Again and again, I treated his virgin dick with true mouth pleasures."

"He was lying on his back, in the middle of his living room, receiving – what to him was – the greatest personal treatment that he had ever experienced with another human being! And that human being was another man! And, this was with somebody that he had only known for a very short time. Only hours! I think he was almost in a state of shock that this was happening to him. I really do think he was pondering to himself, the major question of wondering if he actually had been wanting this to happen to him, for a long time now, and had he mentally blanked that thought out, or was this really something that he had truly never, even sub-consciously, ever thought about?"

"All of a sudden he must have kind of shook himself out of his self-contained bliss of comfort and joy and almost screamed, 'Oh, Jimmy – pull off! I'm gonna cum! Oh Jimmy, Jimmy, I've gotta cum! I've gotta cum!'"

"Instead of pulling off, I grabbed ahold of his body and pulled him up close and tight. I pushed my mouth down that much tighter on his dick! I locked my mouth and his torso together! He was being forced to feed his initial gay cum job right down in my throat. I know he did not expect this to happen, and when it did, he was completely shocked that I, did in fact, force him to shoot his load, straight down in my throat!"

"He started kinda yelling, 'Oh Jimmy! Oh Jimmy! I did not intend to cum in your mouth, but I couldn't get loose from you! You held me so tight and you pushed your mouth down on me so tight! I couldn't get my dick out of your mouth!'"

"I told him, 'Hey Nick! If I hadn't wanted you shooting your cum down in my throat, I would have gotten off of you! Man, I wanted your juices down my throat!' Then I told him, 'I knew, that when I do leave here today, I wanted to be taking part of you with me! Now, I know I am! I've got your first gay play 'boy-shot,' deep down inside of me! Nick, I wanted it! That is the first time that you've ever shot off in a guy's mouth, right?'"

"He told me, 'Oh man, I have never, ever, in my whole life ever played with another guy! I've never even touched a guy's dick before, and I've never

ever had a guy touch mine. Jimmy, I've never, even as a kid, ever had a guy play with me. You are the only guy that has ever done anything to me. Seriously man, I can't believe you let me cum right in your mouth like that. Oh, what a total experience! You know, now I see why gays do what they do. Man, that whole thing! Starting with you on my back – then your hand going up in my ass crack, and then you sucking on my dick!' Then he asked if we could stay in touch with each other so that we could do that again. He said, 'And like real soon!'"

"After he re-coped a little, we got up and gave each other a hug. I looked at him and asked, 'Nick, you just told me that you have never touched another guy's cock before, right?'"

"He told me, 'Yeah, you're right. I've never been in a situation where that's happened. I have to admit, that until today, I'm not sure I ever thought I wanted to, but please – can you pull yours out so I can just see it and touch it? All I want to do today is just see it and touch it. I want us to get together again, real soon, and then I'll try to play with it. Okay?'"

"I told him, 'Yeah, that's fine with me.' And with that statement, I dropped my shorts and let my dick, and my bag of big balls, fall out."

"He looked at my dick and my balls and then slowly reached for my dick. Then he said, 'Man, you have a big thick dick don't you?' Then, as he cupped my bag of balls in his hand, he continued, 'You have got really big balls, don't you? My gosh, man! I think your balls are about twice the size of mine. Do you guys chew on each other's balls? Has anybody ever tried to chew on them?'"

"I told him, 'Oh yeah. A lot of guys have. It feels really good if they can get both of 'em in their mouth and chew on 'em. Then I asked him, 'You gonna try that – when we get together again? Are you wanting to do that?'"

"He said, 'Oh yeah! I think I want to! Yeah, yeah, I guess yeah, I want to, but I've never done anything like that before! Hey, before right now, I've never even touched another man's dick! I want us to get together again. But please understand, I have never ever done any of this stuff, and I may have to take it kind of slowly. You're going to have to teach me a lot of stuff – if you will. Man, after today, I am willing to learn, but I might just need some time to be able to do what I know you must think is easy. Oh, I still cannot imagine that you ate my cum today! Hey man – thanks for doing that. I think that means a lot to me right now!'"

"After he got done handling my crotch of equipment, we both rather put ourselves back together, picked up the towels and the skin cream and discussed how and when we could get together again."

"He told me, 'Jim, I have to admit that if I had ever thought anything, about something like this happening today, I would have never brought you to the house, or let you know where I live or anything about me. I just had no idea that anything except us watching a football game together was going to happen. I never even wanted to try and have sex. I hadn't even thought anything about if maybe you were gay or not when I invited you to the house. I did not know anything like this was going to happen until you put your hand up in the crack of my ass. Oh, that was something I never guessed would happen, but oh man, I am so glad you did that! Oh that felt so good! When I asked you to give me my back a massage, I never, ever thought about anything like this happening. I hadn't even thought any possibility about you and I having sex together. You know I've got my family to worry about, and all of the people that we know, and I told you that I work out of the house, so I can't give you my phone number, but I hope you know where I'm coming from. Is that okay with you? Do you understand, man?'"

"I told him, 'Yeah, I do completely – I do understand! Us gay guys, we have that to deal with quite often. And especially, when we meet some guy at a breakfast cafe place!'"

"I handed him a card from my wallet and told him, 'This is my personal card. It's got my house address, my e-mail address and my cell phone number on it. You feel free to contact me. Hey, I gotta tell you, the whole reason I was out just driving around this morning was because I am single, horny most of the time, but by myself. So whenever you can, contact me. I want us to do this again, real soon.' Then I said, 'Oh hey, wait – your family is gone till Monday, right? Hey, can we get together tomorrow, sometime?'"

"He said, 'No, I'm really sorry. I wish I could, but I just can't do it tomorrow. Sunday is not going to be a good day for me. But I will talk to you on

Monday or Tuesday, so we can get together. But, we'll get together at your place – I assume? Right?'"

"Then, just as I was getting ready to leave, the telephone in the house office started to ring. He turned to me and quickly said. 'Hey guy, I've got to go get that! Can you let yourself out? Thank you so much for everything, man! I'll talk to you real soon!'"

"He gave me a very fast peck on the cheek and then turned and ran for the office and the phone. I turned to let himself out, and just as I opened the side door, I heard my 'new found friend' Nick, answer the phone – 'Hello, this is Reverend Hamilton.'"

CHAPTER 4

Resuming the Walk and The Talk

"Hey, we were talking earlier about where you can hang your certificate, I agree that might not be the right type of certificate for on the company wall – but, what about in your playroom at home?"

"Well, as you might have noticed, I really do try to keep that room, just kind of looking like a normal workout room, unless you're familiar with the stuff and know what it is used for, or happen to look in the drawers and the cabinets. I'm trying to keep it looking kind of that way just in case somebody happens to see in there that I don't expect to be in there. I know that when you, or somebody like you, looks in that room, you'll see the fun stuff. You kind of know what you're looking at, although to most people they'd just think it's an exercise room. I hope anyway!"

"Now, as you damn well know, if anybody opens any of those drawers or cabinets, or maybe notices that the hooks holding those plastic plants are really a very strong type of hook, for those fake plants, then they might wonder about that room. When I set that room up, I really wanted to use that other bedroom since it's a little bigger, but decided that maybe I had better use that smaller room since it's more centered in the house, and if things get noisy in there, maybe the sounds won't carry outside as easily."

"Well, hell!" Jimbo commented. "If I remember last night very well, we sure weren't very quiet in that other bedroom. There was some major pig squealing going on in there!"

"Yeah, there was! But remember the time of night. Everybody living within two blocks of me had been in bed for probably four hours by then. I really doubt that anybody was out walking the streets at that time of night. But, I do have one guy, that lives kind of close, that I do really think would like to know more about what goes on in my house than he's ever told. Knowing him, he might be out walking the street late at night when he knows I have somebody here. Hell, as far as I know, he might just stand outside and listen. You know, now that I think about it, I wonder if he does do that, or ever has!"

"Yeah, why you say so?"

"Oh, he's made a lot of comments about different people and vehicles that he's seen at my place. He's always had a lot of interest in just what's going on here. If somebody seems to be here more often than maybe somebody else, he'll kind of ask questions to try and figure out if I've got a steady or what's going on. I've noticed before, that during the next day, after I've had a late night fun session here with some guy, he'll make comments like, 'Cory, you look tired today. Did you have a good night's sleep last night?'"

"Does he know you're gay?"

"Oh, yeah! He knows! He always tells me when he reads something in the paper about gays. He always wants to talk about gay issues. I've always thought, ever since close to about the time that I moved in here, that he'd play around if he ever got the chance. I'm so damn glad that his house doesn't face my house. I just know that if he could see my place from his, he'd be watching what is going on at my place all of the time. He'd probably just happen to show up at the front door every time I have somebody here. I'm so glad he can't see my house from out of his windows! But, before you even start to ask, would you play with Mr. Dough Boy? Or maybe Santa without his winter clothes on? Okay, does that answer your question before you ask it?"

"Sure does man! Don't even think I have to ask it anymore!"

"My biggest fear with that guy is that I might find him in a gay bar some night and have to actually act like he's part of the community. Maybe what I should do is kind of jokingly mention to him someday, that I have no idea of what in the world I would ever say to his wife if I happened to see him in one of 'our' bars sometime. Hopefully that would make him stop and think about going into a gay bar."

"Uh, yeah it might, but don't think I would wanna to use that approach! I think I'd just keep hoping that he stays away."

"Yeah! I know what we'd like to do once in awhile, is far from what we actually do. Well anyway, I can now comfortably expect him to start asking about you in – oh, I'd say probably in less than a week or so. If he sees you or your Jeep at my house more than twice, the questions start. 'Oh you have a new friend? Are you and that new guy getting serious? When will I get to meet your new friend? Are you and your new friend becoming partners?' Well, actually, he calls lovers and partners, roommates! I've tried to tell him that lovers and partners are not roommates, but he won't listen or change. I guess that's a hangover from the old days. You know back then, if two guys lived together for forty years, everybody thought, and said that they were just roommates!"

"Yeah, thank God things are changing! Maybe we don't think the changes are going fast enough, but thank goodness they are changing at whatever speed it is! You mentioned his wife. Do you ever see her?"

"Oh yeah! Oh my yes! She is the 'Mother' of the neighborhood! Never have to worry if I am going to have any dessert on the table for a holiday. She nurses and babies everybody in the neighborhood as if they were all her own! Since I'm a guy, she is totally convinced that I have no idea of what the oven or the stove are even intended for. She brings me so much food, so that I don't starve, that I have to take part of it over to Mom and Dad's so that it can get eaten before it goes bad. I never let her know if I am planning anything special. If I mention that I'm having some company, she insists that she fix something and bring it over so that we'll have something to eat. Hey, I can't complain, but damn it, once in awhile I do kind of wish she would maybe ask first! With her, it's always a necessity!"

"Hey, my man! Sounds a whole lot better than having folks around that make real trouble for you. Right? Too much food has never been too much of a problem for most folks! Right?"

"Right! You are right! Oh! I can't hardly wait until you really get to know ole Jessabell!"

"Jessabell? Is that really her name?"

"Yeah – Jessabell and Herman!"

"Oh shit man! Are you kidding me?" Jimbo was laughing as he asked. "Really? Jessabell and Herman married to each other? Oh gawd man! Do they have any kids?"

"Yeah, but I think something went wrong there. They have a son and his name is William, and the daughter's name is Jane. Don't ask me! Have no idea! I guess they didn't let their parents get involved in helping name the grandkids! That's the only explanation that I have."

"Hey man, we're doing pretty well trashing the neighbors, but we ain't doing too much talking about ourselves. I thought this walk was gonna be so we could talk about us, and what's happening. Are we avoiding ourselves on purpose, or what?"

"No, I don't think so, but I do kind of think that both of us would just kind of like to just let things continue, and not have to do any thinking about the hows, the whens and all that shit! I know for me, I'm just riding it high, and I'd rather just keep my head there without any real thinking!"

"Yeah, me to." Jimbo responded. Then with some humor in his voice, he continued. "But we have things to discuss like, who's room are we going to fuck in tonight – who is fixing breakfast tomorrow – what day of the week do you do the laundry, and all that stuff."

"Wait, wait, wait! What day of the week do I do the laundry? Is that what I heard? Oh man! Already I'm the wifey? Oh – wait – I am the one that rather likes to get it stuck up into me, ain't I? Well, I guess considering that, I just might have to start being called the 'Mrs.' of the family!"

"No! No, Mrs. Crap in this family! Just us two macho men! But, what are your ideas on things like which place do we spend most of our time at, and which bed do we crawl into at night? All that type of stuff! Cory, maybe I need to ask if you're feeling the same way that I am, and I'm not going off the deep end here someplace. I know that we haven't even known each other quite a full day yet, but I truly do feel that something very powerful brought us together, and regardless of what other hot looking guys are out there, I am just so completely convinced that we are supposed to be together. Do you feel the same way, or is it just me?"

"No, it certainly is not just you! I do agree! I also feel like some higher power overtook the both of us yesterday. You know, when you even think through the rational part of it, why, just why, did you decide to just go get in your Jeep and start driving? Why did you come all the way down here? Why didn't you just go to one of your usual places? I take it, that this part of town is not really your normal area, right? Why did I decide that I just had to get out of the house and try to see who was around? Why did I decide to wear those damn tight jeans that I hadn't on for months? Why did I think that David was going to be of any help to me, in finding someone? Hon, there are just too many, 'whys,' that to me, just cannot be explained, except for the one big explanation that we can only accept, but never explain. And that is it! For some big reason, something decided for us that yesterday was the day for us to finally meet each other, and that force, or whatever it is, followed through! Now, it's up to us to either accept our fate, or be really stupid and not even give our future a chance – although so many things point out to us, and for us, of what we should be doing! Do you agree?"

"Yes!" Jimbo, answered. "And I like the way you kind of explained it too. That is just about the way I would have tried to explain it, if I could have. I know a lot of people are going to think we are way off base by claiming to be together so quickly, but I think, that, it's up to you and I to decide if it's right or not. They're not us, and we can only listen to ourselves. Right? Agreed?"

"Do agree! We may be going into a relationship that is way too unusual for most people to understand. If they do or do not, that's not for us to worry about."

"Okay Cory, I think that right now, all we need to really decide is like, which place are we gonna spend most of our time in? You own your house, and I don't. In-fact, I don't even know which place I'll be living in as soon as Mom and Dad find out if they have a new renter for the house when school gets started again. I've been living there temporarily anyway. What I think we should do – is keep renting the house, and if Mom and Dad find a new renter, then not move back to Fieldcrest. Since Mom and Dad have been great in letting me live there pretty cheaply, we'll keep it and keep it taken care of until they have somebody else to move in. We can kind of sleep over there part of the time, maybe a couple of times a week so that the house doesn't look empty to anybody. Is that okay with you? Do you think that'll work?"

"Yes, I think that is a good way. Obviously, I don't want to think about selling my place right now, but you are right, we can't just move you out of your folk's place. We can continue to take care of it until they find a new renter. Then, we'll just use one place. So tonight we stay at Leaf Lane, right? Hey, I'm not going to refer to that house as 'my place,' so whenever I refer to it, I'm gonna to refer to it as 'Leaf Lane.' Okay?"

"Hey, I like that! It may not be fair on my part, but I do have to agree, that for you to call it "Your Place," would always make me kinda feel like a visitor!"

"Okay, important stuff now! Do you have stuff at your place that you'll need tomorrow morning, before you go to work? Like, maybe your really short, cut off, short-shorts? Since you got the company to change their pants policy, I sure wouldn't want you to go to work with long pants on! What time do you need to be on the job site, and what time will you need to leave the house? Damn, I'll bet I'll have to start getting up earlier than I am used to, won't I?"

"Well, I need to be on the job site at 7AM. I'll have to figure out how long the drive time'll be, from Leaf Lane, and then decide what time you'll need to get up, so that you can get me up on time! Okay?"

"Get you up!?" Cory almost screamed back at him. "What in the hell do you mean, get you up?"

"Well, if I'm not mistaken, you just happened to be the person that I remember hearing you tell David on the phone, that it takes – what did you tell him – it takes five times to get me up? I sure don't wanna ruin my reputation, now, do I? Oh hey! When we get back to the house, I think you oughta call David and fill him in on what is happening with the two of us. I mean, he is part of the reason we found each other, right? If you hadn't been going in that door to talk to him, I would never have seen you. Right?"

"Yeah, you would! I don't know where – but because of all of the things that have happened, I am now totally convinced that if you hadn't seen me go in there, we would have found each other someplace else! Fact is – I wonder just how many times we have – maybe – just almost, found each other, but then something just missed."

"Oh, you too uh? I was wondering the very same thing. I think we need to sit down sometime soon and discuss where we've each been recently. Wouldn't it be a total hoot if we actually did realize that we have, in the past, just barely missed each other for some weird reason?"

"Yeah, but if we did actually find some time when we could have met – that might be just a little too weird for me to handle! When we get back to the house, I'll call David, but I'm not telling him that we're gonna be spending our "First Day Anniversary" in the playroom – starting on the process of seeing if I can get part of my hand up in your ass."

"Good," Jimbo said, as he rather lowered the volume of his voice so that nobody else could hear. "I was wanting to remind you that, I did want to spend at least some of the time today with you playing with my ass. I had already decided that I wanted to always be able to say that you started getting my ass opened, on our first day. Hey, "First Day – Fist Day!" I kind of like that!"

"Well, I know I'm not actually going to get my whole fist up in there today, but at lease we'll start on it, okay? Yeah, right on, my big man! Your ass, my fist, Ohhhh – I like the idea of that!" Cory grinned! He felt that to get his fist up into Jimbo's ass would be kind of like him getting Jimbo's dick down his throat. Just about the same fit, he figured. He had decided that getting that dick down his throat was as tight of a fit as getting his hand up in Jimbo's ass will be. A tight fit that he was really getting anxious to feel!

Cory suggested that, maybe after they get back to the house, they should take a drive up to the other house and get whatever Jimbo would need for work the next day, and maybe check in with Jimbo's parents, so that they could be given the new information about where Jimbo will be spending a lot of his time.

"Yeah, I really do need to pick up some clothes for work and get the job keys. I can call Mom and Dad, but if it was really important to get in touch with me, they've got my cell phone number, and I haven't heard it ring, so I guess nobody's tried to call. While I'm there, I'd better remember to get my lunch box, and then on the way back we had better stop at a grocery store so I can pick up some lunch type stuff. Okay?"

"Yeah, that's okay with me. What type of stuff do you put in your lunch box? Maybe I've already got some stuff at home that you could use."

"Well, usually it's stuff like cold cut meats, some cookies or crackers, a banana or apple, or anyway some kind of fruit, and of course my coffee thermo."

"Hey if some meat loaf and some canned fruit is okay for tomorrow, we've already got that at the house, and I'm sure there has to be some kind of cookies around there somewhere. Hell, maybe Jessabell has even dropped off some at our front door while we were out this morning!" Cory laughed!

"As long as she don't make something like anchovy cookies. I don't even know her yet, and I can about imagine she makes some funny food! Hey man – the meat loaf sounds good to me. That way we don't have to worry about the grocery store today, then do we?"

"Nothing that I need to get that I can think of. I really try to just get everything while I'm there, about once a week. Grocery shopping just is not my bag of tea!"

"Mine either! I guess we're going to have to find ourselves some cute young shopping boy to do that stuff for us! Kind of like having a cute young house boy! Maybe we can get something new started! Instead of guys asking, 'Oh do you have a house boy?,' they'd be asking, 'Oh do you have a shopping boy?' Maybe we should start a new company that finds employment for our new 'Shopper Boys!' Think we could make any money at it?"

"No, I do not! I personally think it would be like the Nude Maids. As soon as the 'maids' found out who would hire 'em to do the cleaning in the nude, then they just had that guy hire 'em directly, instead of going through an agency and giving them part of the cash. If that is what happened – which I can only assume happened since I never hired one, nor worked as one – everything would have worked out for both sides. The nude housekeeper could get paid more, and the hiring guy didn't need to pay as much."

"I don't really think everything worked out so well for – everybody."

"Well, why do you say that?" Cory inquired.

"Uh, well what about the former hiring agent that originally got the two together?"

"Oh! Shit! I kind of forgot about him! Yeah, guess things didn't work out so well for him, did it?"

"Well, that certainly was a quickly considered business plan and a quickly rejected business plan, wasn't it?" Jimbo remarked. "Guess we'll have to come up with some other great plan to make our first million on, won't we? That one certainly didn't pay off!"

The morning walk was a very relaxing opportunity for the two men to simply spend some time together, and not feel any pressures of attempting to make a good impression, on the other guy. They had already accepted the fact that, although, it was still within the first day of their relationship, that they did belong together, and now the pressure was off. Looking over toward Jimbo, Cory just kind of slid sideways toward him as if to bump him sideways a little and just smiled. Jimbo knew that had been an action of attraction and repaid the action, by taking a limp jab at Cory's shoulder. Each man deeply smiled at his partner, and each expressed his love and affection without even saying anything. This unspoken action was very comfortable to each man. It gave them each the acceptance of just walking and not talking.

The path around the lake was long enough that to walk it at a slow pace, it usually took about an hour or more to make a complete circle of the lake. The pathway was quite narrow and not quite wide enough in a number of places for two individuals to walk side by side. More than once, they had stopped at one of these narrow spots and offered the pathway to the companion. First Cory would take the lead, and then Jimbo would take the lead. The switching back and forth became a matter of principle with each man. A number of times, each man attempted to get his companion to take the lead out of turn, and at that time is when somebody, possibly watching from among the bushes, would have wondered just what in the world was going on. Neither man would move. He, either one of them, or both of them, would simply stand there until the appropriate person finally decided to take his deserved position of being the leader.

An observed opportunity of stopping, rather quietly, and watching a mother duck tend to her flock of six very small ducklings, gave them a very enjoyable few, quiet, intimate, minutes together. As they stood on the shoreline and shared the feeling of love that the mother duck was showing to her small brood, they completely disregarded their previous mannerisms of not showing too much physical attraction, happening between themselves. As they stood there in complete silence, each man, as if on cue, reached out for his new sole mate, and the two men quietly stood there, with his arm around the waist of each other. They each turned, looked at his, "new man," and smiled! Once again, as if on cue, they each pulled the waist of his partner closer to himself, so that he, 'he' being Cory, or 'he' being Jimbo, brought the other man closer to himself.

"I like that!" Cory remarked as he watched the mother duck keep her brood in close to herself.

"I do too," responded Jimbo. "Why do I kind of feel like she and her little ducklings are starting out on a new and exciting life just like you and I are today? She kind of keeps the little ones up close to her, and that's what you and I have been doing today, too. Kind of pulling each other up close!

Feeling better and maybe safer, up close. Wanting the other one right there, up close, and within reach."

"So true! What a great feeling to have, too. I just hope Mother duck is as happy as I am today. I hope she has as much hope for the future and all of the good days ahead, as I have."

The comparison between the two tall grown men and the swimming Mother duck and her ducklings was very remarkable, and very comparable, at the same time. To compare the size of the men and the ducks, seemed as something that could not even be possible. Entirely too different, to even consider comparing! Two very tall young men, one man – Cory – stood six foot two and weighed about a hundred and seventy five pounds. The other man – Jimbo – stood about six foot one and weighed about a hundred and ninety pounds. The very little free swimming creatures, swimming so aimlessly in the lake, could have weighed hardly anything at all! Ounces! Far, far, less than a pound each. And their size was so very, very minimal. Especially when compared to the size of the two handsome young men, that were completely mesmerized by them and the expressed love, showing so strongly from the Mother duck. To even think that both types of living beings, the very small lake inhabitants, and the quite larger humans, could possibly be sharing almost the same thoughts, at the same time, concerning somewhat the same things, seemed almost totally impossible. But it was, in-fact, truly happening. Each of the men had conscientiously realized, that phenomenon was taking place, and they were being an internal part of it. Mother duck had, and was expressing, the same love and concern for her new brood, keeping them in line, close and safe, in the very same manner that the two grown men were doing with each other. They, as Mother duck was doing, were wanting to keep the other person in a safe straight line, and watch over him as if being his new mother, much the same way as Mother duck was doing for her new brood. Mother/child relationship, compared to a man to man relationship, is very different, true, but still very much the same with the emotions and concerns of wanting the best for the other! To realize that they were actually experiencing the same feelings as a very small family of simple ducks, swimming freely in a lake of water, was a very moving experience for each man.

"I am having a very unusual experience of realizing that we are very, very, much like Mother duck and her small ducklings, right now." Cory quietly told Jimbo.

"Me, too, my man. Well said! I know exactly what you are saying! I am feeling the same thing right now!" Jimbo whispered as he pulled Cory up closer to himself, and leaned over and gave him a gentle kiss on the cheek.

Cory quickly looked around to see if anybody had seen the kiss. Seeing nobody, and now feeling more comfortable in their possibility of being by themselves, Cory then turned Jimbo's face toward himself, and gave him a lip to lip kiss.

"Hey, my man, if anybody sees me kissing you, and they don't like it, that's their problem, not mine! Right?"

"Right you are sir! I refuse to go through life acting as though I have no feelings for another person, and if it just so happens that my feelings are for another man, instead of a women, so shall it be! They, whoever 'they' are, will just have to get over it. I won't tell them how to run their lives, and I sure don't expect them to tell me how to run mine!"

Cory and Jimbo gave each other a very long and strong armed hug and continued to quietly stand on the edge of the lake, watching with much interest in how 'Miss Mother Duck' and her small six little ones were doing. They watched patiently as Mother duck guided her new family along the shore line until she found an area low enough for her younglings to be able to get out of the water, and it was there that she directed each of them onto the dry land. She had given them their time in the water, and now it was time for them to rest.

Jimbo leaned toward Cory and said, "Hey babe, if at any time I ever say something like 'Mommy and her six,' that just means that I happen to be thinking about this pretty little white Mother duck and her six little new ones. And, I'm thinking about the great feelings I am having right now, while you and I are standing here, arms around each other, deciding how we are going to live our lives together. I just feel so very, very close to you. And I don't mean just the kind of close of touching each other. There is some other type of close that I feel right now, and it's not the physical kind. It's some type of emotional close that I don't know how to describe."

"Hey sweet little thing – I have exactly the same feelings, and knowing that you're feeling the same way, is starting to kind of get to me. We can either get back to walking, or you are going to have one big slobbering crying fool standing here – with my arms around you – and people really are going to wonder – if they see us! This talking is just getting way too deep in me, and I guess it would be tears of joy, but do you really want to explain to somebody why the idiot is crying all over you and himself?"

"I guess we'd better start walking then." Jimbo responded. "I'd sure hate to have to tell someone that I jokingly hit you in the stomach and you just couldn't take it!"

"Well, you snot! I would like to think that maybe you could have made up something a little more damaging and hurting to me, like maybe I got hit by a truck, than that you just hit me in the stomach! You must think I am a real wimp, uh?" Cory asked with a quizzical grin on his face.

"Oh, yeah! A real wimp! And with what I know that you let guys do to you and to your ass? The things that you let be done to you back there, the stuff you let guys put up in there, I don't think I'll ever call you a wimp – well that is until I can take more than you can. Then watch out man!"

The humor of the comments brought both men back to a more normal emotional feeling, and helped each of them shake off the deep emotional feelings that had rather brought both of them down.

"Yes, and speaking of that, I think we should be moving on. We've got some stuff to get done today before we retreat back to the house, lock all of the doors, pull all of the blinds, turn off all of the lights, and start getting nasty with each other again."

"Oh, wow! I think maybe we need to walk faster, then don't you? Uh – what do we have to do today, love?"

"Well, we need to, first of all, worry some about some lunch, if we're going to keep our strength up for our personal bedroom activities, and then make sure we're all ready for going back to work tomorrow."

"Lunch? We just had breakfast didn't we? What time is it?"

"Well, we had breakfast before we came out for the walk, but we started about 10 o'clock, and it's almost 11:30 now. Which reminds me – we are only a few minutes away from our "first anniversary." If I remember right, it was about 11:55 yesterday when you so manly grabbed me by the arm and told me, 'Man, you are going with me!"

"Oh, right!" Jimbo laughingly responded! "I grabbed you? I don't think so, man! If I remember quite correctly, you propositioned me and told me that you wanted me to go with you. And in addition, I thought you meant for lunch someplace, but no man, you were thinking – bedroom! You really are such a nasty ole man! But oh, how I love it! So what are we going to do to celebrate our, 'first anniversary?' Well if we don't dilly-dally too much, we could drive over to David and Suzie's and tell 'em that we want them to celebrate with us. What do you think?"

"Let's go man. I like the idea of having somebody else to celebrate with us. Maybe we should take a bottle of champagne with us. Oh, Shit! It's Sunday morning! Can we buy any anywhere?"

"Yeah, it's after 10 o'clock. Let me call David on my cell and tell 'em that we're headed that way."

As they started walking on, toward the house, Cory dialed David's number and Jimbo heard the one side of the conversation.

CHAPTER 5

'First Day' Anniversary

"David, are you and Suzie busy? Do you have any orange juice so that we can make some mimosas? Jimbo and I are headed that way! Oh, yeah, hey! If you have any stuff hanging around the house so that if you ever need a late minute present, wrap it in anniversary paper, we're celebrating an anniversary! I know, I know! No, I'm not drunk! I haven't even had anything to drink yet today, but we are picking up some champagne, so get the orange juice ready! Okay? No – J-I-M-B-O! Not Jimmy. We'll explain! We'll be there in just about maybe 15 minutes! Soooo – tell her to hurry up and get dressed. She's about to meet her new 'friend-in-law' and she is gonna help celebrate our first anniversary! Yes – the first day – okay!? Hey get with it man! You are responsible for this get together, so now you are going to, kind of, be the father-in-law for each of us, so start getting ready to have a son-in-law! Well, in fact, two of 'em! Oh yeah – tell Suzie she is now a mother-in-law! Hey, we're on our way! See you in a few! Bye."

"Suzie wasn't dressed yet I guess! So I told him to tell her to get with it. They've got some orange juice, so if we want to make some mimosas, we don't need to get any orange juice."

After quickly getting back to the house, they jumped into Cory's truck and headed for one of the "everything you ever wanted in the entire world," type of drug stores and got the champagne.

"Thank goodness for drug stores," Jimbo commented. "Don't think I have bought anything like cough medicine, aspirins or toothpaste in a drug store for years and years, but thank goodness they have the non-essential stuff like champagne! What a life saver!"

Cory and Jimbo turned into the driveway of a very nice and neat, smaller, freshly painted home with some very neatly arranged flower gardens, out front. David came out of the front door just as Cory hit the horn on the truck as if to say, "Hey, we are here!"

"Good morning gentlemen!" David greeted, as the truck doors opened on each side. Suzie is putting on her make-up, so she's still trying to get all gorgeous for you guys!"

Cory gave David a brotherly hug as he jumped out of his truck, and then turned toward Jimbo and said, "David, I would like for you to meet my new life partner. Well – actually – I don't really think he is new, but I did just find him. I think we've known each other for a very long time, but it took us awhile to actually find each other!"

David broke loose from his hug of Cory and turned toward Jimbo!

"I am very glad to really meet you! You and I kind of met yesterday, but maybe you don't even remember me being in the room. I'm really anxious to find out just what's been happening since that 'kind of meeting.' When I called Cory this morning, I told Suzie that I didn't know exactly what was happening, but I was totally convinced that something really good was happening, and that I knew we'd be hearing from you. So your call wasn't that surprising. Come on in, let's see if Suzie's ready yet. You know those gals. Always got to look their sexiest – even when it's gay guys visiting!"

As they entered the front door, Suzie was coming down the hall from the bedroom area. She reached out to grab Cory, and remarked, "Well, my man of the world – I rather understand that celebrations and congratulations might be in order!" She took Cory into her hug and kissed him slightly on the cheek, and then muttered, "He better be a damn good man, or I will personally kick his ass!"

"Suzie, I am personally, totally and completely convinced that, yes, he is a damn good man! Suzie, please meet Jimbo!"

As Jimbo extended his hand as if for a proper hand shake, Suzie then grabbed it and pulled him closer to herself, and then put her hands around his waist. As she gave him a lightweight, slight hug, she then told him, "Jimmy, ur, Jimbo, ur, whatever, I am very glad to meet you, but I will warn you too, as I told Cory, you had better be a damn good man, or I will personally kick your ass!" She then pulled his cheek down to her height, and as she gave him a kiss on the cheek, told him, "I am very glad to meet you. Welcome to our 'family!'"

Suzie then apologized for not really understanding exactly what to call Jimbo, and then asked for an explanation. David and Suzie both appreciated the actions that Cory and, the former, Jimmy, had taken in finding a name that was more acceptable for them.

Just at about that time, Cory looked at his watch and told them that 11:55 A.M. was quickly approaching and that he personally would like for all of them to have a mimosas in hand, at that specific time. Suzie quickly ran to the dining room and yelled back as she ran, "David get the orange juice out of the refrigerator and I'm getting the champagne glasses. The good ones! The ones that we have never had an occasion to use before!"

"If I may," David stated as he rose his glass of mimosas into the air, "I also feel that Cory and Jimbo have successfully found each other, as most people can never do, and I would like to personally wish upon them the greatest of future in their new lives together, and that they do learn to lean on each other when the time is right, and that they also do learn to hold up the other person, as those times are right also. Congratulations to the two of you men."

"And may I also say," entered Suzie, "that I too experience the feelings of a supernatural existence happening, and I wish to throw upon the both of you, the greatest of futures ever experienced by two human beings!"

"Thank you, both of you!" Cory responded. "I truly do appreciate the both of you, but Suzie – you about scared the hell out of me when you started to make the comments about how to, 'throw upon the both of us.' I thought you were going to throw your drink at us!"

"No, no, my man! Not today anyway. I'll wait until I think one of you is screwing things up, then I'll throw something at you!"

Of course, the normal questions happened, such as the description of the entire day yesterday, (some of that detail was left out), what they planned on doing living/house wise, the family situation about Jimbo's family, (they recognized the Hallbrook name) and the other normal, 'let me know what is going on,' type of stuff.

They expressed their feeling that yes, they too agreed that the new relationship did seem to have a lot of items going for it. Items of a very different type than what most people get to experience, including the straight world.

Cory told David and Suzie that he had told Jimbo about David using his leather outfit for a company party, and then jokingly made a comment that maybe David could go with him and Jimbo over to the Calf's Skin after they got Jimbo some more leather.

Suzie, rather laid the law down, and simply said, "That will never happen!"

With that comment, Cory glanced at David and just said, "Well, I guess keeping you away from those guys would be better anyway, wouldn't it? Once they found out you worked at the athletic store, they'd all be all over you just to get a discount, wouldn't they?"

David laughed and said, "Oh yeah, for all that athletic stuff they buy?" Then he looked at Suzie and said, "Hey Hon! Just think of all of the extra commission that I could earn if I got to know all of those guys over at the Calf's Skin! I could make money if I knew them! I'd like to think that maybe they'd be all over me for other reasons, but I guess not, uh?" He then added, "Well, once they found out that I'm a breeder type of guy, I'd be thrown out of there anyway, right?"

"Yeah, right!" Cory and Jimbo both laughed rather heartily.

Suzie looked at David, grinned, and told him, "Hey Hon, you don't work on commission – remember?"

Jimbo complemented David and Suzie on their house and how nice it looked. He found out that they had only been in that house about a year and a half, and they explained their plans of what they wanted to do, with the house, in the future. David told Jimbo that since they had enough property on the east side of the house, that he was hoping that maybe they could build on a couple of additional rooms before they became parents. He also commented, that if he was going to add on before then, that he thought maybe he had better get on the ball, because, "She's talking more and more like a mother all of the time. And she always wants to stop and look at the baby stuff when shopping. Do you think maybe she is trying to tell me something?"

Both men agreed that "Yes, she is trying to tell you something!"

After visiting for about an hour or more, and also taking advantage of the fact that Suzie had just fixed some lunch salads and sandwiches just before they called, Cory then suggested that perhaps they hit the road and get something accomplished. Suzie jokingly apologized that – no, they did not happen to have any emergency gifts hanging around the house, as it had been jokingly suggested that perhaps they might. But, if they could and would come back Friday evening, she would fix them a super supper as a substitute gift. Cory exclaimed, "Oh wow, a triple S!"

The remaining three looked at Cory, then looked at each other, and then David finally had to ask. "Excuse me, but what in the hell are you talking about man?"

In a rather huffy and proper mode, Cory jokingly asked, "Well don't you see? A super supper substitute! A triple S! Isn't that something like a winning horse race bet, or something?"

As Cory reacted like well – how very simple that is – the other three each shook their heads in disbelief and David simply said, "That's okay Cory. We know life is rough for you. You will be okay. You just need rest."

Cory and Jimbo then each accepted the invitation with joy, and Jimbo added, "Yes, we would love to and thank you for the invite. That truly does make me feel like I have been accepted as part of Cory. Thank you very much! What time should we be here, and what can we bring?"

"Can you be here by about 6, and since I have no idea right now at all about what we will be having for dinner, I have no idea of what to bring. I know – bring whatever wine you two prefer, and then we'll have some wine before dinner. We'll make it a formal evening, and if I can get David to build it fast enough, we'll have our after dinner coffee or our after dinner brandy, in the formal parlor!" She then leaned toward Cory and asked, "Hey Hon, is that giving enough impression that he's marrying into class?"

"Hey, honey, let's not over do it, okay? I don't want to make him think my friends are all goofy, okay?" Cory laughed back at her.

After Cory and Jimbo left David and Suzie's, they then drove up to Jimbo's house so that he could pick up the stuff he needed for work the next day. While he was at the house, he discovered that he had a message waiting on the house phone for him.

"Damn, it's Mom and Dad's number. Why can't they just call my cell phone? Let me see what the message says." Jimbo called the message number and listened for a moment.

"I've gotta call Mom." He relayed. "Give me a moment, okay?"

"Well, yeah, of course!"

As Jimbo called his folks, Cory was now the one that could only hear the one sided conversation.

"Hi Mom, it's Jimmy, how are you? Yeah, I know. I didn't stay here last night. I was a guest, at a friend's house. Mom, you have my cell phone number, why won't you use it? That's one of the reasons I have it, okay? No Mom, it's just like calling a regular number! It's nothing but a different phone number, okay? Hey Mom, tell you what! I know how to get you to use that number! I will not be here at the house as much from now on. So if you wanna call me, that is the only number I am going to give you until you get used to using my cell phone, okay? Yeah, well I met a guy by the name of Cory yesterday, and we get along real well. Yeah, yeah. I know. Hey Mom, I'll fill you in later. Okay? Oh –? Like at what time? Hey, Mom, can I call you back in just a few minutes and let you know if we'll be there? Okay, let me tell Cory what's up and then I'll call you back. Okay, I'll call in a few minutes. Bye."

"Mom and Dad are having a backyard cookout this evening and would like for us to come. Bob and Dick and their families are gonna be there. They're getting together about 5:00. Would you like to go?"

"Well Hon, I really think that should be more up to you. Do you want to? Are you ready for all of them and me all at once? What do you want to do?"

"Actually, yes – I do want us to go. I think this is another one of those funny things that is happening for us that is an unexplained phenomenon. It's not that often that all of my family gets together. Usually somebody, Dick, Bob one of the wives, Dad or I, have to be out of town or busy, and for some funny reason everybody is here today for this get together. I feel like this is another of those unexplained mysteries. This get together wasn't even planned until sometime last night. Mom tried to call me last night, but, of course, did not call the cell phone. Cory, why – oh why – was this not planned until after you and I got together? What is happening? Why are these rather funny situations happening? Hey, I don't care. It's working! And it's okay with me! If it's okay with you, we'll go, and we'll use this opportunity to let you meet everybody all at once, and let them meet you, and it'll give us the chance to just let them know what is happening. Okay?"

"Man, if that's what you want, it's quite okay with me! You just let me know anything that I need to know, so that I fit in, okay?"

"Okay, we'll go. I'll call Mom back and let her know. Oh, you know what? We're gonna have to explain the Jimmy/Jimbo thing! We'll get to that after all of the meeting confusion is over, okay? Like when we're just having conversation, then we'll get into that? Is that alright with you?"

"Gawd yeah! I have the feeling that the initial meeting and all of the questions up front is gonna be enough at first. We don't need to change your name quite that quickly. As besides, we've already had one experience today of finding out how many questions can flow, just by talking to David and Suzie!"

"Okay, I'm gonna call Mom." Jimbo phoned his Mom's house. "Oh, hi Dick! You and Terrie there already? Which porch? What did they do to it? So are you painting it all by yourself? Well hell! If anybody had let me know, I could've helped! Orange!? I hope to hell you are kidding!!!! Shit man, you scared the hell out of me there for a minute! I know Mom gets some crazy ideas, but shit I was afraid that what you said was for real. Hey, tell Mom that Cory and I will be there for dinner. Yes – it is Mr. Cory Walker! Dick, you know me better than that! No, it is a guy! And a damn good looking one. We are finally going to have a good looking man in our family! I know it's going to be kind of a rather big surprise to everybody, but we are going to use Mom's cookout as kind of the family announcement that there is a new person in the house, so add to the Christmas list, okay brother? No – well, yesterday! I know, I know! Well, how long did you know Terrie before you two were inseparable? Well – see? Life decisions don't always take a lifetime to decide, do they? Hey, we'll fill you all in later today after we get there, okay? Mom knows I'm bringing somebody, but kind of let us tell the rest of the family, okay? Hey – remember I knew about a week early that you had gotten Terrie her ring, and I never told anybody – right? Okay, keep your mouth shut then – okay? What? Oh, hi Terrie! What did he do? Give you the phone so he could go finish painting? Yeah, I'll be there and I'll be bringing somebody very important with me.

Yeah – you'll like him. We'll fill you in on everything when we get there – okay? Don't tell anybody else yet – okay? Oh, hey, Terrie? What should we bring? Well – what if we stopped at a bakery and picked up a cake for dessert? Would that be okay? It's not going to be home baked, but it's a cake, okay? Alright, will do! See you before five. Bye."

"Dick and Terrie are already there. Dick is repainting a side porch that they put a new floor on. Okay, here's the run down. I certainly don't expect you to remember all of it, but the list is, Dick and Terrie. One son, and one daughter. The boy, Junior, he is like about ten years old. Actually his name is Richard too, so that's why he's called Junior. And then Becky is about six years old. Then there is Bob and Barbara. Sometimes they are just called B&B. They have one daughter. She is Stephanie, fifteen years old. Dick is all excited about me bringing somebody. Terrie's all excited and anxious to meet you, too. Oh yeah – I told 'em that we'd pick up a cake for dessert. Don't let me forget."

"Well, let me see! I guess while I'm still here, I should find something decent to wear. I'm gonna wear a new pair of shorts that I bought but have never worn, and some kind of a pull over T-shirt. Something like that okay with you?"

"Yeah, man! Like, this is your family, not mine! As long as you don't ask me to wear tux and tails, anything is fine. You know my good man, my tux and tails just happens to be at the cleaners since I wore 'em to the castle gathering the other day!"

"Oh right, your highness! I forgot you spilled your pudding all over the crotch of your tux the other day didn't you? Well, pudding — so I am told! Sure did not look like pudding to me, did it? But it sure was nice of that man servant to attempt to clean it all up by licking it clean for you!"

"Oh, yes! You can always count on the castle staff, you know?"

"Oh, Yeah-right! The castle staff! I think it's a bit more like the Calf's Skin staff. Right?"

After Jimbo gathered together everything he needed for work the next day, plus his desired wear for this evening's cookout, they then checked the house to make sure no water was running or any extra lights were turned on, and then headed back to Cory's place. Or, as they had agreed to refer to it – Leaf Lane.

"Okay, it's now about 2:30 and we need to be over there by five, right? Oh hey, we have to stop and get a cake someplace too, right?"

"Oh shit, damn it! I wish I had remembered to stop and get that on the way here so that we don't have to remember it later. Shit! Why in the hell did I forget it? Hey, if we ran over to the Calf's Skin for a quick afternoon cocktail, is there a decent bakery someplace around here where we could pick up one on the way back?"

"Yeah Jimbo, there certainly is! There's a bakery called Caker's Bakers, real close. They have absolutely fabulous cakes! A lot of weddings use them for the wedding cakes. They know who I am. I could call over there and see what they have available, and I could ask 'em to hold whatever we decide on, and then pick it up a little later."

"Wow, sounds like a damn good plan to me! Hey, I know Becky doesn't like chocolate, so lets avoid that, and I guess about anything else is do-able. Give 'em a call and see what they have. I guess they must be open on Sundays, right?"

"Yeah, they're in the shopping center over here on Brown Street and they're open until about 5 or 5:30 on Sundays. They'll be open late enough for us."

Cory called the bakery, and the phone was answered by Sharon, the owner. "Sharon – this is Cory Walker. What in the world are you doing in there this afternoon? – Well, is she okay? How long till she can come back to work? Okay, now listen, if you get in a real mess over there, you know I can work the counter for you. I can't do too much back in the bakery, but I sure can count cookies! Okay, now remember, I'll help if you need me. You can't work seven days a week and not get sick yourself. You hear me? Okay! Oh, yeah! What cakes have you got available? Oh wait! Jimbo, how big of a cake should we get?" Jimbo told him one big enough for about twelve to fourteen people, and Cory then relayed that to Sharon.

"Jimbo, Sharon said she's got a yellow cake with white icing that size. Is that okay with you?" Getting Jimbo's confirmation, Cory then told Sharon that they would be picking it up in a couple of hours, reminded her again that if she needed him to help, to give him a call, and thanks for holding the cake.

"I'm going to call my folks and tell 'em that I am going to be busy tonight so that they don't wonder why I haven't called 'em or stopped by this weekend. I'm not going to get into a conversation about us. We'll go over to their place sometime this week and introduce you, okay? After I get off of the phone, do you still want to go over to the Calf's Skin for a couple?"

"Yeah, let's do. I might as well start feeling like that is my home bar too. Besides, I might run into some more of the construction crew. Right?"

After Cory phoned his folks and had a short conversation with his Mom, he and Jimbo then changed into the clothes they wanted to wear to the family cookout, and then headed out for the Calf's Skin.

CHAPTER 6

Sunday Afternoon at the Calf's Skin Bar

The bar was not too overly crowded. Sunday afternoon did offer a rather different selection of men than the late nights did, though. And the bar was much more relaxed about the dress code. The Calf's Skin had an outside patio that was built to resemble a cattle corral. The normal and usual Sunday method was to stop at the main bar inside, get a drink and then head on out to the corral. Cory and Jimbo rather naturally followed this unspoken ritual. The corral was a rather large sized space with its own serving bar that had about ten stools at it, and a number of old western style tables with built on benches.

As Cory and Jimbo came out to the corral, Cory said, with a rather surprised tone in his voice, "Well, I'll be damned! There's Billy! Hell, I haven't seen him around here for months. Come on, I'll introduce you to one of my co-workers."

"Billy, what in the hell are you doing in here today?" Cory asked as he slapped Billy on the shoulder.

"Well, hello man!" Billy responded as he turned, saw Cory, and then rather quickly looked more toward Jimbo and sized him up one side and down the other. "How in the hell are you today, and all I can say right now is – I just hope to hell, that the longhorn walking beside you, just happens to be here, and is not really with you, right? And if he is with you, I sure do hope he is flexible with who he spends his time with! I've seen some pretty good looking cattle in here before, but I think the meat grade has just been moved up to U.S. Prime Grade A!"

"As horny as ever, I assume uh, Billy?" Cory jokingly asked.

"Well, until just right now, I didn't know that I was horny, but shit man, when a guy gets to look at something like that, don't tell me that even a straight guy can keep from getting a little horny for it! Does the man have a name, and please tell me that he is not really with you!"

"Yes, he does have a name! But hell, right now I'm not so sure I want you to know what his name is! Billy, this is Jimbo. And yes – he is with me! And no, you may not touch! You may shake his hand, but then you get your hands the hell off of him!"

As Cory put his arm around Jimbo's waist, he informed Jimbo of the alarm about Billy. "Jimbo, Billy is one of those guys that your Mother always told you to watch out for!"

"Hello Billy. I'm pleased to meet you. Cory mentioned that you two work together, right?"

"Yeah, yeah, yeah, work – that stuff! Let's not be concerned about that right now. Work talk – later! Right now I've got to find out when in the hell the cattle truck hit town and why I was not informed so that I could have gotten the pick of the herd! Jimbo, let me tell you about your friend Cory. He's a plain old bitch. I'll bet he has had you hidden in his closet and keeping you all for himself, hasn't he? He never shares his toys. He's the kind that will say, 'Well it's my ball and I am going home.'" As he turned and looked toward Cory, he continued, "Well are you going to share your toy today, man?"

"Hell no man, especially not with someone like you! You are way too anxious to get your crummy paws on him. I won't even let him get close to you! Which reminds me. Where is your better half today?"

"Oh hell, he's out of town for a week at a conference. So now you know why I'm so damned horny! It's been three days already without anything up in my ass, and I think it's growing closed."

"Oh, so that's why you were acting so bitchy Friday when I saw you? I thought maybe the ole man got on you about something that you did wrong. I didn't realize that you had been put out to pasture for awhile. Damn, I'm sure going to stay away from you at the office this week! If anybody says anything about you, I'm just going to tell 'em you're on the rag, and stay away from you. So when does he get home?"

"Not until Wednesday night. And all I can say is that he had better be damn horny when he gets off of that plane, because I'm going to rape him right there in the terminal!"

Cory turned to Jimbo and said, "Jimbo, remind me to stick one of those bigger dildos in my truck tomorrow morning. I think maybe we have a friend that just might need to borrow one sometime soon so that his hungry ass doesn't get him in trouble at the airport. Sound like it to you?"

"Hey man, you know how we always need to take care of our brothers, and this brother sounds to me like he is in a real big need. Anything that we can do for him, I guess!"

Billy looked at the two and remarked, "Thanks men. Shit, I'm in a real need here, and all you two can do is offer me a hunk of plastic or whatever those things are made out of? I need something more than that! But, hell I can tell – all of my crying on your shoulders is not gonna do any good, so just tell me where in the hell you managed to find this hunk of meat, and just make me feel bad that you're the one that always gets all the good stuff."

"Right, all the good stuff! Jimbo, don't feel sorry for that little cry baby! You will get to meet Shawn, and when you do, I think you'll agree with me that Billy needs to just shut the hell up and enjoy the hunk of meat that he gets to go to bed every night. His partner is a coach at the Community

College, and he fits the roll. Shawn is a damn good looking hunk, and why in the hell he has this thing – well, let's not even wonder about that!" Cory remarked as he grinned toward Billy and squeezed his shoulder. Cory continued, "Mr. Billy – Jimbo is now my other, and better half, and the how we met, you will never believe!"

Cory and Jimbo then related much of their last thirty some hours to Billy and explained to him the new lives that they were looking forward to. Although Billy had been rather smart ass acting when the two came in, his mood certainly did change to a much more serious tone as he heard what had happened within the last day. He expressed his complete joy at the new relationship. Billy said that he was really very sorry that Shawn was not there to celebrate with them, but even in his absence, Billy insisted in buying the two new lovers a full bottle of champagne as congratulations. Being in the corral, champagne was not a drink often asked for out there, and especially a full bottle, so it did take a few minutes for the bartender to get a bottle for them, from the main bar.

As the cork was popped, and the glasses were filled, Billy stood up on the stool, that he had been sitting on, and announced. "Gentlemen of the corral – I would like to introduce to you, the 'Mr. Cory' and his new husband, 'Mr. Jimbo.' Or maybe the husband thing is the other way around, but none the less, help me salute them and wish them the very best in their brand new relationship, which is now only about one day old. Congratulations men, and the very best to the both of you!"

As Billy finished, actually almost everybody in the corral, something like maybe 35 guys, all raised their drinks and yelled. Nobody is quite sure what they yelled, but they did make a loud uproar. Cory and Jimbo hugged each other and waved back to the crowd and yelled their thank you's! At this point in time, and with this happening to themselves, they were very glad that they had come back to the Calf's Skin for a Sunday cocktail. This afternoon was turning out to be much more exciting than either of them had expected it to be. As they continued to talk to Billy, others would stop by and offer their congratulations and best wishes. This truly did make Cory and Jimbo very proud of the men that they were associating with.

"You know." Jimbo said. "Gays are supposed to be such a weird group of misfits in society – but you know – I think we would have trouble finding any other group of men that act as nicely to each other as this group has been toward us today! Billy, thank you so very much! This has been just great! Another one of those funny things that has happened to, or for, Cory and I since yesterday. You happen to be here today, and you said it's been how long since you were last here?"

"Well, I think the last time I was here was when they had the Man and His Toy Boy Contest. What – last January?" He asked as he looked toward Cory.

"That's right!" Cory chirped in. "That was the time when those three or four guys were trying to get you and Shawn to enter the contest because they thought you were his boy."

"Yeah, right! Thanks for reminding me! Maybe that's why I've not been here since then. I didn't want to be reminded that I acted like I was his 'Boy.' Gawd! For weeks after that Shawn kept calling me 'Boy' whenever he wanted me to do something. I finally got him to stop by calling him – 'Old man!'

"Is he older than you?" Jimbo asked.

"Hell no! He and I are the same age. We're both thirty two. Well, he's like three months older than I am, and I really played that up to him when he kept calling me, 'Boy.' I like the playing around stuff, doing roll playing, but not all of the time. Just when it's in the bedroom."

After they managed to finish off the bottle of champagne, Cory and Jimbo decided that they needed to be hitting the road so that they weren't late getting to the family cookout. They explained the get-together to Billy, and Billy expressed his complete joy that they were going to have that chance, so early, to introduce Cory to everybody. The three gave each other hugs, and they then started toward the door. Once again they were interrupted as they left the corral, and then also in the interior bar, with men that came up to them and congratulated them on the new relationship.

After finally escaping the bar and all of the well-wishers, they stopped by the Caker's Bakers and picked up the cake that Sharon had set back for them. Cory introduced Jimbo to Sharon and checked with Sharon, to make sure that with her worker out sick, that Sharon was making it okay. Once again Cory insisted that if he could help her out in any way, to give him a call. She promised that she would if she needed to. She sincerely thanked him for offering and then looked at Cory and with a smirk on her face, added, "You gay guys are just too much! None of my other customers have offered to help me, if I need it! Thank you Cory!"

That comment made both guys feel very good, and both very proud that Cory had offered. It also paid off with a half dozen warm fresh baked cookies that Sharon gave to them for being so nice, as to offer.

CHAPTER 7

The Hallbrook Family Cook-Out

As the Jeep turned into the driveway of the Hallbrook home, Cory let out kind of a low, "Wow!"

Jimbo knew why he had done that and reminded Cory that, "The family is in the business of building houses, remember? You really don't think we can express our business by living in a real small house, now do you? It actually looks bigger from the outside than what it really is."

"How big is it? How many bedrooms are in it? Does your Mom have house help to help keep it up?"

"Cory, it's not that much. It's only a four bedroom house and no Mother does not have house help. We just ain't that fancy of a family. If Mom and Dad are having some type of a fancy get together, then she'll have some help, but other than that, it's usually just us kids that help out. Now don't start acting like you're going someplace way too fancy. We're just normal, common everyday folks."

They parked the Jeep, and because of the house, Cory kinda checked out the cars in the driveway, looking to see if there were any, real fancy, expensive, cars there. He decided that maybe Jimbo was right. Maybe they are just a normal common type family. There were no fancy cars at all. Just the regular stuff like everybody else drives. Now he felt better.

"Mom! Hi, how are you?" Jimbo asked as he got out of the Jeep and gave his approaching Mother a big hug. "Mom, I want you to be the first one to meet Cory. You'll be seeing a lot of him in the future."

"Cory, this is my Mother. We call her, 'Mother Hubbard.'"

That remark deserved a little fake slap from his Mother, and her comment, "Yeah, and we call you Goofy. So Cory, you can see, none of us take the other ones very serious! Cory, I am very glad to meet you. Come on inside guys. Everybody is here and we are just getting ready to take the stuff outback. Dad is lighting the grill, getting ready to burn up some steaks. Cory I do hope you like beef steaks!"

"Yes, yes, I certainly do!" Cory responded, but at the same time wondered if Jimbo's Mom was actually thinking about the same type of beef steak that he was. He wanted to, so badly, tell her that he had found his beef steak yesterday! "Sounds very good to me. Oh, Jimbo, the cake is in the Jeep!"

"Oh gosh! I forgot about it too. Guess I was too anxious to give Ole Mother Hubbard a big hug. Hey, hang tight, I'll get the cake."

"Jimbo?" Mrs. Hallbrook asked. "Is that what you called him?"

"Oh, yes I did. I wasn't supposed to do that until we had a chance to explain, but I feel he is a little too grown up to be called Jimmy, so he said he liked 'Jimbo.' So that's what I call him. Okay?"

"Yeah, it's okay with me! You can call him anything you like, I usually just yell, 'Hey you' at him."

Jimbo introduced Cory to everybody in the house, which did include both of the brothers, both of the sister-in-laws and the three kids. His Father was out in the back yard, so they then went out back to introduce Cory to his Father.

"Well, it's about time you got here, young man!" Jimbo's Father exclaimed.

"Why? What do you mean? And – oh, yeah, Hi Dad! Glad to see you too! Dad this is Cory."

"Hi, Cory, glad to meet you. Now Jimmy, I need help with these steaks. Your Mom always accuses me of burning 'em, so I hope you came with your cooking gloves on, man!"

Mr. Hallbrook then turned toward Cory and with a grin on his face, told Cory, "Young man, you just never get done raising your kids, or trying to learn how to do stuff right for the wifey!"

"Cory, if you haven't yet noticed, my folk are always so glad to see me. They're so glad that I show up, and as soon as I do, they throw a shovel or a broom or something in my hand. I guess today it is the cooking stuff."

"Okay Dad, so what're you planning on doing while I finish your cooking for you?"

"Well, young son. I intend to take Cory off to the corner over here and tell him all of the trash about you that I can think to tell him, so that he really knows what he's getting involved with if he's going to associate with the likes of you!"

And with that, Jimmy's Father handed Jimmy the Bar-B-Q tools, put his arm around Cory's shoulder and continued, "Come on young man. We need to talk!" Mr. Hallbrook then turned toward Jimmy and laughingly gave him a grin.

"Cory you only believe about half of what Dad tells you, and then disregard about half of that too, okay? Dad, you keep our dark deep family secrets to yourself, okay?" Jimmy hollered as his father and Cory walked toward the back door of the house.

"Cory, I noticed that nobody bothered to either give you a beer, or even show you where we hide 'em, so let's go get ourselves a cold one. Oh! And if you ain't no beer drinker, you are in the wrong house! Understand?"

As they came into the kitchen, Mrs. Hallbrook and the two daughter-in-laws were getting dishes and food ready to be taken out to the patio. Bob and Dick were at the kitchen table nibbling on everything that the women sat down on the table.

Mrs. Hallbrook asked them to, "Please remove yourselves, gentlemen! You are in the way, and you are eating all of the food before it's even put on the table."

Mr. Hallbrook handed Cory two beers and suggested, "Here, I'm sure Jimmy is ready for this too – since he's out there working his butt off so very hard. Oh, and when you go out, tell him not to burn those steaks! Tell him to not to take over any of his Dad's bad stuff!"

Cory returned to the patio and handed Jimbo his beer.

"Hey did you notice that when we got here and I remembered the cake, I accidentally called you Jimbo instead of Jimmy? Your Mom asked about it, and I just told her that I thought you were too old to be called Jimmy and we decided on that."

"Oh! What'd she say about that?"

"Nothing really! She just said, 'Okay.' Then she told me that she just usually yells, 'Hey you' at you. She didn't seem to be bothered at all!"

"Well, I guess it's okay with her, at least then, ain't it?"

Just at about that time, Jimbo's Mother and the grandkids came carrying out some of the food and dishes. Cory offered to help set the table, and get things ready for eating.

The meat was getting very close to being ready, the table had been arranged, all of the food was on the table and everybody was standing around doing small talk. The conversation did come up about Jimmy using the Jimbo name, and everybody kind of accepted it as an okay to them. Jimbo's Dad did make a joke about how Jimmy is his youngest and will always be a little boy to him, and that changing his nick name wasn't going to change anything in that regard to him. That's when Barb reminded her father-in-law that it was on their wedding day that Bob asked the family to quit referring to him as 'Bobby.'

"That was the day he told the family, 'You know, now that I'm a married man, I think I'm now old enough to pass on the 'Bobby' name, and move on to just being Bob.' And Dad, you respected that, and so I think we could respect Jim's wish too! Everybody agreed?"

Everybody agreed that yes, Barb was right and that from this point on, Jimmy would now be 'Jimbo.' The family had made a unanimous decision!

"Thanks everybody, I appreciate that and I now do feel older! Do I look any older?"

"Well, Mr. Jimbo," his father asked, "What about at the company? We're changing it there too?"

"Hey Dad, most of the guys there just call me Jim anyway, so I don't think we will have too much to worry about there, and if anybody does call me Jimmy, I'll just tell them that I'd prefer Jimbo. I think everything'll be okay. Oh, Dad! Do keep making my pay-checks out to James, though! Okay?" With that remark, all of the adults chuckled and laughed.

As everything was getting set up and ready for eating, Cory did notice that for some reason or another, he felt that Dick was kind of trying to stick pretty close to him. He pondered the why! To find out if there was some reason – or was this completely his imagination – Cory managed to kind of separate himself from the main group by walking over toward a fish pond as if to check it out. Sure enough, Dick quite quickly followed him and stuck up a conversation. Cory was only slightly nervous about this happening. He didn't have any reason to even slightly understand why Dick did seem to want them off separately, but at the same time, Dick had certainly come across to him as a very friendly type of guy, so he didn't worry too much about it.

During the small walk, they did look at the gold fish in the pond and maintain a conversation of no specific importance. Then the real, true, conversation rather started to come to light.

"I kind of like and agree with Jimmy about getting people to call him Jimbo instead of Jimmy. Why did he pick that name, do you know, Cory?"

"Well Dick, I really don't know. I just know that I told him that I personally would rather not call him Jimmy, since I felt that it was way too juvenile for him, and I asked him what maybe I could call him. After he thought about it for a few minutes, he just told me that for a long time he has always kind of wished people would call him 'Jimbo' instead of Jimmy. I asked him where that came from, and he really didn't know. Why do you ask?"

Cory specifically did not mention the conversation about the possibility of somebody calling him that at a young age.

"Well, Cory. The real reason that I am kind of curious – there used to be a guy in our neighborhood that was like about my age, and we had noticed a few times of how often that guy was always around when Jimmy was there, and yes, I did hear him call him, 'Jimbo' once. So when the Jimbo name came up, it really made me wonder just what might have been going on back then. He never mentioned Joe, then, I assume?"

"Well Dick, he did mention that guy, but didn't call him by name, and I do know nothing funny was happening between them though. When I asked him why that name and he did not know, I did ask him if maybe somebody had called him that when he was little, maybe somebody that he kind of liked. That's when he did wonder if that guy, the one you said was Joe, had called him that name, but that he didn't remember it happening. He said that he always remembered Joe just calling him something like, 'hey you!' Maybe that's where it came from, because Jimbo did admit that he really did like Joe, but he certainly didn't give me any type of a hint that anything at all had happened. I'm really sure that if it had, Jimbo would have told me. Especially during that specific conversation. Dick, I wouldn't worry about it, and if anybody else in that family mentions it, I'd just tell them that Jimbo just liked it better and to him it sounded more mature and grown up, than Jimmy."

"Okay, I just wanted to find out from you if I could, because I have personal reasons to know just where Joey was coming from, and I had always wondered too. Hell, maybe Jimbo and I are now old enough to be able to talk over stuff like that between us now. In the past, it's always been avoided. Hey, thanks Cory. I'm glad that even though you and I have just met, that we feel free enough with each other that we can have the kind of conversations that I have always felt like I needed to avoid with Jimmy. Hey! You know what, I think I just gave myself an understanding of why I felt I needed to avoid those conversations with him.. I just called him Jimmy, didn't I? Now that he's Jimbo, now, maybe I'll feel like he is old enough to treat differently."

"Oh, okay. You feel like you and I can have open conversations, right? Got a question for you, then! You said that you knew where that Joey was 'coming' from then. Meaning? I took that as you either know or really think that Joey was playing around with other guys? Is that what you were saying?"

As Dick looked around to make sure nobody was approaching or within hearing range, he continued, "Yeah, Cory, you know how young kids do stuff. Well, he and I did the typical teenage experimenting a couple of times. I kind of moved on, but I know Joey rather stuck with his new experiences. Hey, Cory, I'll tell you, maybe Joey just was not the right person to show me what could be exciting on that side of the fence. I mean, hey, I'm not even so sure Joey ever needed under briefs to hold anything in place. Know what I mean? See, knowing that Joey was doing the guy thing, that's the reason why I had always wondered if anything had ever happened between him and Jimmy. But, hell I just couldn't ask. Then when the Jimbo name came up, it really made me wonder again."

"No – I'm just totally convinced that if anything had gone on between 'em. Jimbo would have had no reason to keep that from me when we talked about him. I'm convinced that nothing ever happened. Whatever happened to this Joey guy? Do you know?"

"Well no, not really. All I know is that the family closed the Barton Furniture Store and I guess his folks retired kind of early. I guess they must have done very well in the furniture business. Whatever happened to them, I really don't know."

"Wait, wait! Barton? His last name is Barton? He is about your age? Not a real tall guy, maybe like about five feet eight or nine? Blonde hair, or used to have?"

"Whoa – sounds like maybe you know him? Do you?"

"Hell yes! He's still around! He's now a banker. Not as much hair on the head now, as I would guess he probably used to have. Almost bald! He's very active in the biker community. So the banker thing and the biker thing, makes for a very interesting combination. Seeing him in the bank, you would never vision him as a biker. And on the bike, you'd never vision him as a banker! With a shirt and tie and a suit coat on, you never get to see all of the tattoos he has all over his body and arms. I see him, oh I don't know, maybe once every other month or so. It'll be interesting when Jimbo and he run into each other again. Hell, I wonder if Jimbo'll even recognize him or not. I'm sure he looks a hell of a lot different now than he did as a younger guy! I guess he was never a very athletic guy, right? Like never worked out or did much of anything very active?"

"Yeah, when I knew him, about all he did, as far as I know, was read a lot. He never played ball with the rest of us or anything like that! Didn't keep the body in shape, I presume?"

"Good way to put it, my man! Well, I guess that goes to show that the gays from the downtown area and this area don't get together very often. Hell, I'm surprised that Jimbo hasn't seen him since he's been back in town. I need to set that up sometime without letting Jimbo know, and see what happens. Damn, this could turn out to be funny!"

"Keep me informed, okay? I'll be interested to see what happens. Okay, now another question since we, as new brother-in-laws seem to be getting along pretty well, uh, I – well assume that you and Jimbo have at least showered together, right?"

"Uhhhh – yeah – Dick, we are gay guys! What are you getting at – may I ask?"

"Well, there's something about the Hallbrook guys, and I was just kind of wondering if it followed through with my kid brother or not. We had a little too much age difference between us for us to do too much showering together, so I just never found out. You know what I mean? You know what I'm getting at?"

"Yes, Dick I sure as the hell do! And yes, I guess Jimbo can rightfully carry the Hallbrook name. If he didn't have the Hallbrook attributes, then I wouldn't know what in the hell you were talking about, would I?"

"You're right. If he didn't have the credentials, you'd be wondering just what in the hell I was referring to."

"Okay, man. You got basic with me to find out. Now I'm going to get basic with you to find out if I'm with the right Hallbrook or not. He's at ten and about a half. As his older brother did you use up too much of the Hallbrook thing, or is my man the bigger of the subject?"

"You did okay man! Hey, I really don't know for sure how long mine is. You know us straight guys don't get into that measuring thing as much as you guys do, so I've never measured it before."

"Shit, don't give me that shit man! You know as damned well as I do, you straight guys are as interested in your sizes as we are. That's the reason you even mentioned Jimbo's dick! Hey, if you've never measured it, or don't know how, don't ever say you've never had somebody offer, to measure it for you." Cory said, as he gave Dick a very large grin!

"Okay, I'll never tell anybody that – again, that is! May shock the hell out of you, but just might take you up on that offer, sometime!"

"Great! Like the suggestion of that! Something we should not mention to Jimbo, I assume?"

"Hey, let's keep this whole conversation just between you and me for now anyway! Okay? If we expand our conversation, let's do that after you and Jimbo have been together for at least a couple of weeks. I'm not trying to take his man, but I think you'll find out I'm not the prude of the world either. This just happens to be something that came up between you and me. Jimbo and I have never had this type of a conversation before. Okay?"

"Got you man. Just you and I. Hey, I think maybe we'd better get back over there before I have to make up too much conversation to explain what we were talking about."

As everybody was lining up and filling their plates with all of the good cookings that was now ready and available, Jimbo asked Dick, "Well – what have you two been out there talking about?"

"Oh, I had Cory out there showing him the prize winning gold fish that Mom has. Kind of also filling him in on the fact that if he is around here very often, he'd better have some work clothes stashed someplace, because Mom and Dad always seem to have something that needs to be fixed up or painted, as I found out this weekend. Which reminds me, does everybody like the new paint job on the side porch?"

Everybody quickly agreed that it looked just great to them, and Dick then told them that of course they all thought it was pretty damn good, or they each knew that if they didn't like it, then it was up to them to re-do it.

After a couple of refills on the dinner plates and doing all of the normal small talk that will happen when a family has a good dinner together, everybody rather agreed that for right then, they were all pretty "damn full!" Complements were fast and furious as to how good everything had tasted.

Jimbo then offered to show Cory around the inside of the house, and to show him the projects that had taken place and been accomplished, since the house was originally built.

As they entered the house, Jimbo told Cory, "Hey man, you may not be too interested in this, but at least I figured it would get you and me away from the rest of them for at least a few minutes. And besides I want to know what you and Dick were really talking about out there by the fish pool. I know damn well it was not just the damn fish! He has never cared about those fish ever since Mom had the pool put in. What did you guys talk about?"

"Small talk, really. He just kind of talked a little about you wanting to be called Jimbo instead of Jimmy, and stuff like that. We'll discuss it all later, okay, man?"

"Uh, okay, I guess!" He answered, as he gave Cory a look of query, as in, "I really do think there is a whole lot more to this than is being stated!"

"Hey, since we are on the official tour, this is the part that got added first. Dad designed and built this house so that about each time it was added onto, it was a new and larger living room that got added, and the older living room was converted into something else. It's been added onto about four times. Hey, come here. Let's go up here and I'll show you the best addition that they did."

As they climbed a set of stairs, they entered an obvious bedroom.

"This is the only addition that was not a living room. This upstairs bedroom was added for me. They added this room when I was like in the eighth grade. And if you'll follow out here, I'll show you the sun deck, where I used to get my nude suntans."

"Nude suntans? Is that what you just said?"

"Yeah! When they added on this upstairs bedroom, putting on this sun deck above the garage was a natural. If you look around, you can see that nobody can even see you are up here, unless somebody is standing over there in the woods. And if that side bothers you, you can easily put a chair on that side and block that area. This is where I had the nude photos shot."

Cory rather quietly leaned over toward Jimbo and asked, "Nude photos?"

"Yeah, about a year ago I heard there was this photo student that was looking for some guy that would agree to be photographed in the nude, and somebody that also had a good scenic place to take the shots. So, I got in touch with him, and suggested me and this sun deck. I knew Mom and Dad would be gone one weekend, and I had already told 'em that I'd come over and stay at the house that weekend, so everything worked out very well. That guy came over and brought a couple of other hot guys so that we could do some group type of shots."

"Did you do gay type stuff?"

"Well, nothing really too much! But we did do the kind of shots where we were hugging, or have our hands on the shoulders of the other guys, but nothing like grabbing a guy's dick or anything like that. No sucking or

fucking shots. Not that it didn't happen that day, but we didn't photograph
it."

"What type of a photo class was this guy in? Was it a school or what?"

"It was some type of a private class. Not with a school or a college, so I
wasn't too worried if my face was shown or not. He did tell me though that
he was only going to use the shots that did not have clear face shots. I guess
part of his classes was to learn how to do something like that where you only
want certain parts of the picture to really show. I have some copies of them,
but we will not mention them to anybody else. Okay? I really don't think
Mom and Dad would be too happy finding out they had been taken here at
the house."

I think I would agree with that! I am anxious to see 'em as soon as possible
though!"

After finishing the 'official' house tour, and having some cake and ice
cream for dessert, Cory and Jimbo decided that it was about time for 'em
to get going. They extended their thank you's to Jimbo's parents and told
everybody else good-bye and goodnight.

Dick did not react any differently than all of the others as Cory and Jimbo
were leaving, except to give Cory a very strong handshake, and remarked,
"Hey you guys take care." Then looking at Cory, he said, "We'll talk to you
later," as he gave Cory a strong grip, as he finished the hand shake. Cory
felt that perhaps, yes, he did know what Dick was secretly relaying to him.

CHAPTER 8

Going Back Home

On the drive back to Leaf Lane, Cory realized that Jimbo did not have a key to the house, and that he would need one tomorrow. He asked Jimbo to stop at another one of those so very helpful, 'have everything drug stores,' so that he could get a copy made for him. After doing so, both men decided that they each thought everything had been done that they needed to get done, before they went to bed. They agreed that thinking through what was necessary was kind of a challenge, since everything seemed to be so totally different than just two days earlier.

Cory questioned, "Seems to be so different? Hell yes it is! Everything is different!"

They pulled the Jeep into its new parking spot, closed the garage door and then turned and gave each other a very good, long, kiss.

Jimbo told Cory, "Man, I have been wanting to do this all evening long! I guess it would've been okay in front of the family, but I'm not so sure just how everybody would've reacted."

"Well, I know one of them certainly would not have been offended!" Cory responded.

"What? What? Who? What in the hell are you talking about? Cory, does this have anything to do with that conversation you and Dick had? What in the hell are you saying?"

"Oh, I'm not saying anything! I just know that Dick is not too upset with us being together. He's just pretty glad for us, that's all."

"I don't think that is all! I think there is something that you are not telling me, man! I'll get it out of you eventually! You two talked about something that I don't know what it is, but damn, I will find out eventually!"

The two lovers entered the house arm in arm, and again gave each other a hug and a kiss.

"Hey Hon," Cory kind of lowly whispered to Jimbo, as he looked directly into his eyes and rather squinted his nose at him. "Why don't you go on in the bathroom and get your ass all ready and then go in the playroom and stretch yourself out on the bed. Kind of get yourself all ready for me and my hand to come in there and play with your ass. Okay?"

Taking a very deep breath, Jimbo replied. "Yeah, man, let me tell you though, that I'm really starting to get real nervous about the idea of you trying to get a hand up in my ass. I'm not changing my mind, I still wanna go as far as we can, but man I'm not going to kid you any. The idea of trying to take your hand up in there has really kind of got me shaking."

"Hey Babe, don't get scared. We're together! You're safe and you're just gonna get a chance to do something that you've never done before – and I know that doing new stuff can be scary. You go get stripped down and just lie down on the bed. As soon as I get this stuff cleaned up, I'll be in, and we'll take it nice and slow, so that you don't get freaked out, okay?"

"Okay man, but you gotta remember, I don't use my ass like you do, and I ain't used to getting stuff rammed up in there. You gotta remember, my ass is like really, really virgin. I've hardly ever even been fucked before. This is really making me nervous!"

As Cory hugged and gave Jimbo a kiss, he reassured him that he was in no danger, and that everything was going to be okay.

Jimbo did the bathroom 'thing,' then went into the playroom, which did, also, include a comfortable bed in addition to the other 'exercise' equipment – stripped himself completely down and laid down on the bed. As he laid down, the thoughts of a whole hand going up in his ass once again bothered him. He had to reassure himself that he actually had been looking forward to this kind of activity for a very long time. It was fear in the past that had prevented it from every happening, and today he had to overcome that fear. He knew he was now with a man that he could completely trust and who really knew how to do it. So with those thoughts in mind, he attempted to lie back and just relax. And, he attempted to look forward to this new and exciting experience. He thought, 'Hey, guys do this all of the time. If they do it and like it enough to keep doing it, then hell, it must be good or they wouldn't be doing it. I've got to be man enough! I've gotta do it!'

Cory finished cleaning up the kitchen mess, locked the doors, turned out the lights, checked the garage door, and entered the playroom – completely nude.

"Man, oh man! You look so damn hot to me! I want to eat all of you. And I am going to start with that damn big dick of yours. I know you are really nervous about my hand going up in your ass, and I've been acting just a little too rambunctious about it. So I'm gonna slow down and help you get into the mood first. Is that okay?"

"Yeah man, that's good. I think that'll help! I really do! I don't wanna be a wimp, but honestly, the idea of a hand going up in there really does scare me. I don't know why, but for some reason I'm just afraid that doing that will just leave me with a ripped open asshole. Stupid – I know. Hell, you get it all of the time, and a lot of other guys do too, so why in the hell would it be any different for me?"

"I told you about my first fisting. Well, my first attempt at getting it that day – I know I was so damn scared too! But that big muscle boy had me so damn turned on sexually, hell there was no way that I was not gonna go through with it that day! We don't have any big muscle boys here tonight to get your mind swinging all around in circles, but I think that if you and

I work together, you might start finding out that you're a lot more anxious than what you think right now. What I think we should do, to get started, is for you to hold that damn big telephone pole up in the air so that I can sit down on it again like I did last night. Hey, remember how last night I was so cautious on how fast I rammed that thing up in my ass? Well tonight, my ass is just plain screaming for it! Listen –."

Cory rather covered his mouth and lowly yelled, "Oh Mr. Dick, this is Mr. Asshole! I am so hungry! I need to be fed! Please come stick yourself up in me. Feed me please! I am so very hungry for you!"

"Oh God Cory! You are so weird sometimes! Well, I think and assume you are, anyway! That is about the weirdest, that I've seen you get, so far! But – if that's any example, okay! Let me ask you, if your ass is so damn hungry for this dick, is he gonna eat it raw or are you going to put some cooking grease on it? If there's anyway that you think you can get it up in you, without lube, I'd love to try it! Any chances?"

"Hell no man! My gawd no! Now who is acting weird? You think I'm going to get that damn pole up in me without some lube? You are crazy man! Wait – have you actually fucked some guy before without using any lube?"

"Yeah, did once. But, although he claimed that he didn't have any lube up in there, I kind of think that maybe he had just been fucked by some other guy, and that guy left some slippery stuff stuck up in there. It felt like it anyway!"

"Hey, where were you? Why do you think this guy had just been fucked by some other guy?"

"Oh, that was during one of my – not being such a 'good boy' days. I was driving I-10, coming home from Texas and I really, really, just had to stop at the roadside rest and take a piss. You know how often us guys traveling alone always have to take a piss! You know how in those larger roadside rest parks, they have the semis park on one side, and the cars on the other? Well, if you just happen to pull in on the wrong side, kind of like you can't watch where in the hell you're driving, you can, and do quite often, end up having more fun. You get a chance to do more than just take a piss!"

"Oh man, this sounds like a trucker story! Right?"

"Well, I guess I'd have to say – Yes! You see, of course I was very innocent. You do understand that, right?"

Cory looked over at Jimbo and grinned a stupid looking grin, and shook his head yes as he said, "Oh right! Of course! The dear little innocent guy that just never ever goes for it! Keep up the story. I want to hear about the trucker."

"Well, do you want to hear about the trucker on Monday, or the trucker on Tuesday?"

"What? I'm getting confused! What do you mean, the trucker on Monday or the trucker on Tuesday? Oh, did you have two truckers?"

"No, only one trucker. But we kind of had a two day road affair. We kind of found each other rather fun, so as we drove, we fucked, and then we slept then we fucked, then we drove, then we fucked and just kind of spent two days that way."

"Shit man! You mean that you just kept stopping at the same places and getting back together for two days?"

"Yeah, that's right! When we first met, we just happened to both be taking a piss in the rest room. Well, he either pisses very, very slowly, or maybe, just maybe, he happened to be looking for some dick. Well anyway, if he was looking for some dick, he found it!"

"God yes! If he found you, he sure as the hell did find some dick! So –?"

"Well, in the rest room he kind of complained about the lousy paper towels they had in there, and how in the cab of his truck he had some really good thick towels, so that when he needs to, he has 'em available, and he asked if I would possibly like to, maybe, go use one of his towels, since those were so damn lousy!"

"Well, a man certainly cannot, with any dignity, turn down another man's nice generous offer, such as that, without hurting his feelings, can he? Of course not! He certainly did have a very nicely decorated cab on his truck. I have no idea, of who in the world, prints so many nice pictures, of such nicely built guys, showing such nice strong muscled bodies, as that man happened to have hanging in his truck. I don't think, maybe, I was supposed to notice 'em, but hey, you know once a piece of art is noticed, the only polite thing to do is to compliment the owner on it. He seemed very pleased that I did – just happen – to notice the prints! Anyway – back to the fucking! Yeah, he got fucked! In the cab of his truck! Yeah, right there in the roadside rest area, and the first time I rammed it into him, I didn't even ask him if he wanted or had any lube. I just aimed it and rammed it. No problem! It went in nice and smooth and quick and deep! But the next time, his ass didn't seem to have quite the same amount of 'slideability' as it did the first time. I think he had just been fucked by some other guy, just before I got to him that first time. I think his earlier fucker had lubed up the inside of his ass, and it was still there and available for me to take advantage of. Oh, yeah! I certainly did, too! Made the cab of that semi rock and roll! Hey, at one time I really was getting kind of nervous about all of the motion and noise that I really was afraid, might be coming from the cab of the truck. When I mentioned it to him, and suggested that maybe we needed to calm down some, he told me, 'Hell man – that's the best way of finding some of the best sex on the road. Some of the hotter guys do watch for cabs that are either moving or giving off a little noise, and then they'll knock on the door and ask if they can come in.'"

"Now some of the drivers don't care if you're humping a guy or a gal, but some of the guys only want one of the two varieties. And let me tell you, it's really fun when it's a Highway Patrolman. One that's only checking to make sure everything is, 'okay!' Just wanting to make sure there's 'no problems!' They'll often suggest that they really should report any unfavorable activities that happens to be going on – but if – well, maybe there is a way to overlook it this time! He told me that he has had some really good sex with some of those officers. See, most of 'em are married guys, and they keep their eyes open for as much activity as possible, whenever they can. I guess they like both sides of the fence, so to say! He said that if it's after dark, and you get a knock on the door, you can almost be sure it's a patrolman. After dark is their time! Their patrol cars don't show up so much after dark, and they kind of hide 'em between the big rigs. He told me that he has the phone numbers for five or six cops that want him to call 'em when he's headed their way. They find out just when he's gonna be pulling in, and then they come out to the truck stop and tie up with him for a good dick session. He told me one guy told him that he'd even take a full night off, so they could have sex all night long, if he got the call early enough so he could call in sick for the night."

"So anyway we kept this little roaming road side session going on for two days until he had to go one way and I had to go another. Ever since then, I keep my eyes open a little more for state patrol cars at roadside rest areas. Especially at night! I would love to find a patrol car, then just sit by his car until he crawls out of the cab of the truck and just ask him if there's, 'anyway that maybe we can keep me from reporting this to his headquarters.' Hasn't happened yet, but hey – maybe someday!"

"Shit man! Some guys always seem to have all of the fun! Damn I never get to have that type of a session! Two days on the highway! I sure do hope he was a hunk!"

"Oh yeah," Jimbo quickly responded. "I do think he was probably the hottest truck driver that I have ever seen. So many of them kind of really turn me off. Hell – not that one! Remember, the highway patrol guys had him call 'em when he was headed their way! He must have been one of their best! I don't think he had been driving trucks very long. He looked way too active for that. I'd like to see him again today to see if he's still that hot, or did he get all fat and flabby or not."

"Back to the subject at hand." Cory said, as he squeezed Jimbo's dick. "Let's get some lube on your dick and up in my ass – if we're gonna make believe that you're a semi-truck, oil dip stick, going up into its holder thing."

Cory lubed up Jimbo's cock, and rubbed some lube up inside of his own ass. He then climbed above Jimbo, the same way he had done the night before. The only difference this time was that, his ass was very ready to take that entire ten and one half inches of stiff dick up in him, and as quickly as possible.

And he did! Slam, bang! It went up and in there, and Cory was fully, quickly, and rambunctiously sitting down on Jimbo's body. Both men let out an expressive, "Oh" at the same time. Same time but for different reasons. To Jimbo, the feeling of his complete dick going up into Cory's interior so quickly was somewhat of a shock and surprise, but was also a feeling of complete joy! For Cory, the 'Oh' rather represented an expression of satisfaction that he had, in-fact, taken that entire thick cock that quickly, without any discomfort, and all of the interior surfaces of his ass were singing all of their praises of joy, for the gentle massage that they were receiving.

Cory's other excitement was knowing that he could now jump up and down on that dick as quickly and as rapidly as he wanted to, so that he could enjoy the complete excitement of having it up in him as far as it could possibly go. The full length of it, the full depth of it!

"Shit man! It feels like a watermelon up in there! Oh shit, man!"

"Damn that feels so damn good! Hang on man! I'm gonna fuck my ass with your dick as fast and as furious as I can, without knocking either one of us out of this bed. The bed springs might be gone after this, but what in the hell do I care now? This is too close to like the time that big guy tried to get his fist in me for the first time. Hell, my ass is so damn hot right now that all I can say is, I hope to hell the house is not on fire, because right now I'd just yell, 'Burn baby burn! Fuck me! Damn – fuck the hell out of me Honey! God! Make my ass raw and sore! Shit man – fuck me hard – real hard – real hard!"

Cory was almost at screaming levels with his excitement of Jimbo's dick up in his ass and his own personal action of getting as much action back in that ass as he could. He rather forgot in all of his excitement that he was the one in control, and not Jimbo. Jimbo was rather flat on his back, and did not have too much opportunity to get involved in the fucking activity, except for his pleasure of fucking Cory's tight, and obviously very hungry ass, without actually have to move too much.

As Cory was yelling for him to fuck his ass really hard, Jimbo could only question, 'How in the hell can I fuck him any harder, he's the one on top! Whatever action happens up there is all his doings. He's got control of this situation, all I can do is lie here and keep a stiff dick.'

Cory's activity, solidly perched on top of Jimbo's dick, gave him an automatic climax. He shot his wad from Jimbo's belly button, up across

Jimbo's chest, across the side of Jimbo's face and onto the pillow that Jimbo had under his head.

"Shit man! Damn I didn't even have my hand on that!" Cory exclaimed with some disgust.

"Damn man, I didn't want to shoot off that fast! Damn man! Hell, I didn't even feel that building up! Just all of a sudden it was flying out! Crap, I'm not real sure that I have ever shot off that way before. I mean, yeah, I shot off while sitting on some guy's dick, but that's because I was kind of jerking it off! Hell, this time I didn't have either hand even close to it! Hey, Mr. Jimbo, I guess you've returned me back to my childhood days when cumming was like automatic, whenever I happened to see some guy in some small tight Speedo trunks. Shit that felt good! Just did not expect it! Let me get a wash rag and tidy you up a little, then we'll get you turned over and get down to the business at hand. Okay?"

"Yeah, if you still want to. But since you've shot your wad, if you want to pass tonight, I'll understand!"

"No, no, no, man! I know what in the hell you are trying to do. You're trying to find an excuse of why we don't spread the cheeks of your ass tonight. Aren't you?"

"No, actually, maybe it was your action on my dick, but I'm a hell of a lot more anxious now than I was before. I'm still scared, though! Damned scared! But damn, I want it now!"

"Hey, just you relax. Here, turn your face the other way so that I can wipe this side clean. There! Now Babe, you flip yourself over and lie on your stomach. Spread your arms out and just let your whole body relax. Okay?"

Cory laid down beside Jimbo and then reached over to a drawer and removed a rather slender dildo. Jimbo did feel him make the move, but didn't see what Cory had done, but didn't bother to ask, either. Jimbo had finally reached a point where he was now just going to let Cory do his thing, and give his complete trust to Cory and his knowledge of what do to next.

Cory grabbed the lube and spread some on the dildo, and then some on Jimbo's asshole. As he rubbed the lube on his asshole, Jimbo made somewhat of a surprised movement, but then calmly settled down into his relaxed mode again. Cory massaged Jimbo's asshole with his fingers and very gently entered his hole with one finger. Jimbo did react. Cory gently patted his ass cheek with the other hand and suggested once again that he just relax. After a few more minutes of using just the one finger, Cory then inserted another, and continued this action for some time more, until he had successfully gotten three fingers into Jimbo's ass, and without Jimbo making any negative comments. Using the three fingers that were comfortably inside, Cory massaged the interior as deeply as he could reach. He was very pleased to hear Jimbo make some very soothing and comfortable moans as Cory moved his fingers around and felt the interior of Jimbo's ass.

Cory reached over and picked up the lubed dildo and placed it at the entrance of Jimbo's ass. As he removed his fingers, he so very slowly started the entrance of the dildo up, and into Jimbo's ass.

Feeling the something change, Jimbo asked, "Hey, what's happening man?"

"Nothing serious man. Nothing serious. Just taking care of your ole asshole. Just letting your asshole experience the feeling of another man groping around the edges of it, and having that asshole feel some new and exciting things happening back there that have never happened back there before."

Cory continued to insert the dildo into Jimbo's asshole. And Jimbo was actually taking this a little faster and a somewhat quicker than Cory had expected. He was also very surprised that Jimbo was lying there very comfortably and not objecting to anything that was happening back there. The dildo was the smallest in diameter of any that Cory had. He didn't want to freak Jimbo out by starting out with too large or too fat of one. But the way he was accepting this one, Cory decided that perhaps he had picked out one that was, in-fact, just a little too skinny. As he pulled it out, Cory realized that Jimbo had very easily taken about six or seven inches of this stick. More than he had expected Jimbo to take, especially without any comments, since he does not usually get his ass played with.

Cory pulled the first dildo out and laid it across the small of Jimbo's back as he reached into the drawer and removed another 'tool.' As the dildo was being removed from Jimbo's ass, he made a slight moan, and to Cory it sounded more like, "Oh don't take that out," as opposed to a, "Oh, man that feels better." Cory grabbed the tube of lube and lubed up the second dildo. Jimbo knew something was happening back there, but didn't make any remarks or ask any questions. Cory then positioned the dildo at the entrance of the ass and once again ever so slowly started its entrance into the chamber, but on a very slow and gentle path. As the head of the dildo entered into his ass, Jimbo did make a jerking motion and gave out a deep moan. Cory quickly asked, "You okay man?"

"Yeah, I'm okay – but you must have something bigger now, right? It feels really big! I assume that's a dildo you have in me, right?"

"Yeah, it's just a dildo, but yeah it's a bigger one than the one I used on you first."

"Well man, is this one a lot bigger or something? This one feels like it's a baseball bat or something."

"No, it's not that big! Here, this is the first one you had. The one in your ass right now is only a little fatter."

"That's what you had up in me first?"

"Yeah!"

"How much was in me?"

When Cory put his finger down about seven or eight inches from the end, he told Jimbo, "You had this much in you. Down to here – where my finger's at."

"You're kidding, right? You are shitting me, right? I didn't have that much up in me, did I!? No man! I couldn't have had that much up in me. No – if you had put that much up in me, I would've really felt it up in there. That much would have hurt! You probably got, what, one or two inches in me – right?"

"No Jimbo! No, you had this much in you! Why would you think it was only an inch or two?"

"Cory, when that was up in me, it felt good! But I had no idea you had that much up in me! Really, man, what you did back there, then, it really was feeling really good! Did you try to push more of it up in me, or is that all I could take? I never felt any pain like you were pushing on something. Did you try to get more of it up in me?"

"You were taking this one so easily, I decided that I needed to get a thicker dildo up in you. That's why I got this other thicker one."

"Oh shit man! I can't believe it. I've taken that much and didn't even realize something that long was up in there? Oh man – I'm kind of freaked out by that! I thought it was really gonna hurt to get that much up in me. Damn, maybe I really have been missing out on something. Okay – I'll lie back down and try to relax. Now you've got me all excited about taking that bigger one. Hey, if I squeal, don't pay any attention to it. Okay? I guess I really want it now! Knowing that I've already taken that much without any pain, is really getting me all turned on! Hey, Cory, if I squeal, don't pay any attention to it unless I tell you, 'enough.' Okay? That way, if I just make too much noise, it won't matter, but then if I do need you to really stop, then you'll know what I mean. Is that okay?"

"Sounds like a good plan to me. In-fact, I think it sounds like something that we should stick with all of the time. That way we'll always know when we really are expected to stop something – and when we can ignore any squealing."

Jimbo re-relaxed on the bed, and Cory resumed the penetration of the dildo. Jimbo was feeling really pretty good that maybe he wasn't coming across as a wimp, and Cory was feeling very good that perhaps he was helping Jimbo experience some new stuff, that he had never experienced before.

Cory did know that the earlier dildo was a one and a quarter inch diameter, and this additional one was one and three quarter inch diameter. He realized the one half inch doesn't sound like too much of an increase, if stated, but when it's going up in a virgin ass, as it was into Jimbo's, it's enough to make a person, 'sit up and take notice!' Well, in this situation, he knew the sitting up was not really a possibility, but he was certain that it would make Jimbo take notice. And Jimbo did take notice! As Cory ever so slowly pushed it into Jimbo's ass, Jimbo squirmed and moved about on the bed some. His reaction to this dildo was definitely different than his experience was with the first one. This one did give him some interior feelings. With this one, he definitely did know that he was getting something pushed up and into his ass. He never complained about it, nor asked for it to stop, but he definitely did know something was happening back there. Something big!

"How much have you got up in me?" Jimbo did inquire. "How far in is it?"

Cory adjusted his finger and thumb to indicate about a six inch spread. "I think you've got about that much up in you. You really are taking this much faster than I had expected you to! Are you sure you don't get fucked back here all the time, and just don't quite remember it?"

"No, I'm sure I don't get fucked! Hey, Cory I don't know if this is going to sound weird to you or not, and I don't know if you would even go for it or not, but I really do wanna be lying on top of you, while I try getting a fist up in my ass – or at least as much of one as I can. When we try to do that, I'd really like to be lying on you and holding you! Can we do that? I'd really feel a whole lot more safe if I could be holding onto you! I really want you to be holding me tight, real tight, when that happens. Can we? Please?"

CHAPTER 9

George Joins In On The Fun

"Uh, I'm confused. Give me that again! You want what?"

"I wanna get a fist or a really big dildo up in my ass – but while that's happening, I really do want you lying here, under me, so that I can hang onto you, and you can squeeze me if I need some help handling the pain – when I have some. What I'm wondering is, do you have a friend that could come over and put dildos or his hand up in my ass while I get to lie here and hug onto you, and have you hug me back? Whoever is playing with my ass and trying to get me to open it up, is not nearly as important to me, as me getting to hold onto you while it happens. While you've been trying to get that second dildo up in me, I've been wanting to put my arms around you so madly. Hey, with you back there, I can't even see you, let alone hug you! And I was just wondering, if maybe there was a possibility of us doing that?"

"Well, hell, I do admit that is a new idea! I hadn't thought about that. I guess it really isn't important of who's back there ramming it or stuffing it. The more important thing is to get you opened up and help you be able to accept the fact that you can get fisted, and then I can get in back there anytime I want to. Would that make you feel more comfortable if we did that? I'll admit that I like the idea of being able to hang onto you, and let you hug me and squeeze me if you need to. I could help talk you through it better that way too. Yeah, I think I like the idea! No, I really do like that idea! Man, for a guy that claims he don't get too wild, you sure have come up with a super idea this time!"

"Hon, if that idea is okay, and a turn on for you, I'd like to do it. I've been wanting to hug you this whole time you have been working on me with that bigger dildo."

"Do you want me to see if I can find someone for yet tonight?"

"I'd like to if possible. Do you think anybody might be available and willing?"

"Hey, for a chance like this, I'm sure that anybody we ask will be willing if they're available. Let's face it. It's not every day two lovers call some guy and ask him to come and help one of the lovers get his ass opened up! You know, some of 'em just might think I'm the crazy one for asking some other guy to come over here and put his hand up in my lover's ass!"

Smiling over the thought of letting another guy came in and now be an active part of the action, Cory leaned down, licked the back of Jimbo's neck and said, "Hey, I wonder if George is available? I'm gonna pull this out, and go give him a call! If he's available, I think he'd be great! Number one, he's a very experienced fister! He has been the first one in a lot of guys' asses. For some reason he kind of talks 'em into becoming fisters and fistees. Besides that, he's a great guy, and a damn hot looking guy. Stands real tall. Like about six foot five! Long slender hands, but not too wide. For getting a fist the first time, that is important! Let me give him a call!"

Once again, Cory gave Jimbo a quick loving lick up the middle of his back, slid out of the bed, washed up a little and then dialed George to see if he was available.

"Hey, George. Hello. George this is Cory. What in the hell are you up to tonight? I have a very new member in my family – yeah – a partner, and we could use your help if you have some time available for us. Okay, ready for this? I think this is going to be a request that even you have never received before! Jimbo would like to be lying on top of me, while his ass is opened up, either to take a fist, or at least get as close to it as possible. We've been playing in his ass with some dildos tonight, and when I had the bigger one in him, he said that he was wishing he could hug me while that was happening. He just told me, that if possible, he'd like for me to be lying under him so that we can hug each other while somebody else works on his ass, and lets him find out if he can do it or not. I kind of liked the idea! Well hell – I mean I really do like the idea! The idea of having some other guy playing with his ass while I hold him – that really, really, turns me on! Hey, a lover is asking you to come over and play with his lover's ass! Now that is a new twist, isn't it? So what do you think? Hey man – whenever it's convenient for you. We've already been playing some, so we'll just continue till you get here, and I'll have the side door unlocked so that you can just come on in and not have to knock. Hey, when you get here, I might be getting fucked, and I don't intend to come answer the door if he has that big dick of his up in my ass. Oh yeah! Yes – yeah, it's a big one. We measured it last night. Over ten and a half inches long and just almost as thick as a beer can. Choked the hell out of me when I put my face on it. Yeah – of course I've had it up in there, and it fits nicely! Hey when you get here you can see it, and if you do us a really good job tonight, maybe we'll just let you play with it as a pay back. Okay? Okay! We'll see you in, like what, probably maybe fifteen or twenty minutes? Good! Great! I'll keep working on him. I'll see if I can get one of the fatter dildos started in him while we wait for you. Okay! See you shortly."

"Hey, I'm sure you heard. George should be here in about fifteen or twenty minutes. You'll like George. He's a real sweetie. He sounded real anxious to get to work on your butt. Believe me, you are getting one of the best, when you get him! I'm really glad you thought of this idea. Hey, did you know about George somehow or something? Was this a set up for me somehow? George is one of the very few that has fisted me up to the elbow before. And wait until you see the length of his arms!"

"Oh man, this really does make me nervous now! I know bringing someone else in was my idea, but shit, now I'm really getting nervous about it. What if I just can't hardly take any of his hand and this whole thing turns out to be a real mess? George won't think I am a wimp, will he?"

"No love, he won't think you're a wimp. He has tried many, many times to get his hand up in a guy's ass and it just never happened. He knows some guys can take it, and some guys simply cannot. I really think your idea of lying on top of me while he works on your ass will be a good thing. Believe me baby, it will work! We'll make it work!"

Cory and Jimbo settled back down in bed, and Jimbo asked him to kind of keep working his ass with his fingers so that it would open up as much as possible before George got over there. Cory did finger him, and also went back to the thicker dildo that he had previously been using on Jimbo's ass. With a little more grease, and some cautious patience, Cory managed to get a longer length of the dildo up and into Jimbo's ass. More than what had been up there, previously. Jimbo did some squirming around on the bed as Cory slowly forced its entrance, but he never told Cory to stop or to pull it out. Cory was quite surprised at how freely Jimbo was taking the dildos without any complaining. Cory was becoming more and more convinced that once George got over there and got started on Jimbo's ass, there was going to be success to celebrate before the evening was over.

"Oh shit!" Cory exclaimed. "I didn't unlock the side door for George. Hey, you just lie there. I'm going to leave that dildo stuck up in you. Now don't shit it out while I'm gone, okay?"

Cory left the playroom and went to the family room to unlock the door for George. As he returned, he was quite surprised at what he was seeing. Jimbo was lying on his stomach, but had his hand stretched back, pushing, or attempting to push, the dildo farther into himself. Jimbo could not see Cory, so Cory just stood at the door to see, and to watch just what was happening. Jimbo was acting very intent on trying to get more of that dildo up in himself. He was in a very awkward position to attempt this, but he was giving it his all. He was moaning and groaning more than he had been when Cory was working on it. As Cory stood there and watched, he became totally convinced that Jimbo was truly trying to get all ten inches of that dildo up in his ass, and it looked like he was trying to accomplish that before Cory got back to the room. Jimbo had shoved an additional three inches or more of the dildo up into his ass, when Cory finally told him, "Shit man! Leave the room for just a minute or two, and you eat the whole entire thing! Your ass really is damn hungry, ain't it?"

Jimbo attempted to flip his head around far enough to see Cory.

Cory grinned and said, "I will say this about you, young man! I can see your ass really is much more hungry than I was aware of. You just damn near have that whole thing up in you, don't you? Shit man, you should have been telling me to just push harder. I was so afraid that I was getting too aggressive, and hell I should have been really going at it. It looks like we've only got about, maybe, another two inches or so to go to get that big bag and balls base up against your ass! And I think we had better get that done before George gets here, don't you?"

Jimbo didn't say anything. He just looked at Cory and gave him a big smile that rather said, "Let's get it up in there big man! Let's do it!"

Cory put his hand on the base of the dildo and started to push it further in. He had to admit to himself that he was not being quite as gentle with Jimbo's ass now as he had been before. He had decided that Jimbo really was hungry and anxious for this entire dildo up his ass, and he just had not realized that quite yet.

His thinking now was, "Okay man, now I know! Now I'm really going for that ass. My man wants it, and I sure as hell am ready to give it to him! He'd better hang on now, his ass is gonna be full in a moment."

Knowing that Jimbo's ass was hungry, and that it had already taken the greatest part of the shaft and was completely open for the entire girth of it, he told Jimbo, "Here it comes man, you're getting all of it!" And with that stout exclamation, he did fully push the rest of the dildo up into Jimbo's ass! Jimbo did jerk and kind of jump as Cory rammed it in, and allowed the base of the dildo to slam up against Jimbo's ass. Once it was in place, Cory continued to push against the end of it so that Jimbo could feel the pressure of the base up against his asshole. In-fact, he rather hit the outside end of it a few times so that it continued to have a sensation and not be just sitting there. Just as he was pushing on it and asking Jimbo if he was alright, and getting a reassuring that it did feel good to Jimbo to have it all the way up in there, he heard the family room door open and close.

"Hey, we're in the playroom, George! Come on in and look at what we got done since I just talked to you! The guy on the bed, is well – just call him

Jim while you fist him, and then I'll introduce the two of you after we're done. That way 'Mr. .... Jim' will always be able to tell others that he first got fisted by some guy that he hadn't even met yet!"

"And to you 'Mr. Jim' – if you need to speak to the man that is going to be up in your ass, pulling it apart and stuffing more up in there than you ever thought you would even think of – you just call him Mr. George."

"Hey Cory, where's your blindfold? I really think our Mr. Jim should be blindfolded during this adventure so that he can't see me, and if for any reason I should decide to leave before we let him take off the blindfold, then every man he sees for the next few days he can wonder, mmm– is that the man that had his hand up inside of my ass? You know I got fucked in a bathhouse once, lying face down on my partner of the night, when another guy came in, fucked my ass, and I never saw him. To this day, I have no idea of who that guy was, or even what he looked like, that fucked my ass. I've always wondered if I've talked to him sometime, and he knows he's fucked me, but I don't know it. Handsome, ugly, skinny, fat – hell I do not know! The idea though of knowing that some guy was up in my ass, fucked me, and I have no idea of who he is, is kind of exciting to me! Even though that's been a few years ago, the idea of having had some guy up in me, fucking my ass with his dick, and having no idea of who he is, is still a complete turn on and excitement to me. Maybe we should just let Mr. Jim have the same experience. What do you think?"

Cory got the blindfold out of the drawer and put it on Jimbo, or as was now being referred to, during this play session, "Mr. Jim."

"So, although I see Mr. Jim can comfortably take a – what – a ten inch, thick, dildo up his ass, you say he's never been fisted – right? Is this the first time that he has had that size dildo up in there?"

Cory and George rather quickly took to the "arena" of talking about Jimbo as if he wasn't even in the room. To Cory and George, this was something that had just happened without either one of them being conscious that it was happening. To Jimbo, it turned him on. He liked the way he was feeling as if he had become a non-living toy. Something that two guys were going to be using as a toy, and not being a third person.

"Yeah, from what he tells me! He told me that he's hardly ever had his ass played with. He told me that he's never used a dildo on himself before – so when we started with that small dildo earlier tonight, that was a first for him. So what we've done tonight is a whole new experience for him, back there. But George let me tell you, his ass took that one and the smaller one without any complaints. In-fact, when I went out to unlock the side door for you, when I got back in here, he was pushing more of it up in, than what I had put in 'em. He didn't know it, but, I stood there at the door and watched him force himself to take it, and that's when I decided that I was gonna feed the rest of it to him. And man, oh man! Did he take it like eating a chocolate syrup sundae! I really don't think your hand, going up in there, is going to cause nearly as much stress back there, like we thought earlier it might."

"Yeah, let me play with this dildo just a little so that our toy boy can lie there and relax, on it. Then we'll get to the real stuff. Sure does have a hot looking ass, don't he? I like looking at it spread all wide open with a big dildo stuck up in there. Cory this is not the thickest dildo you have, is it?'

"No, I have one that's a lot thicker. It's a three inch diameter at the head of it and has about a two and a half inch diameter shaft on it. It's my big one. I'm not sure you can get the head of that one in him, though. George, that's the one that I have to squat down onto to get it forced up into my ass. I've never been able to get anybody else to get it up in me. Because all of the force that it takes, it just scoots me away from 'em. That's why I have to put it on the floor and squat on it."

"That's okay! We're gonna try it anyway! You guys just lie there, and get Mr. Jim in a good position above you so that you can hang onto him, and he can hang onto you. I assume it's in this cabinet, right?

"Yeah, right! Bottom shelf, George."

"Hey Hon," Jimbo whispered to Cory. "I do understand that I am now a toy, and I am supposed to act like a toy, in other words be played with and shut the hell up, but can I talk to you or do I have to keep my mouth shut then too?"

"No, you can talk to me. That's why we've got you on top of me, so that you can tell me what's happening, and I can be sure you're okay. George is gonna be your slave master for a little while, but I'll be your playmate that you can share with. Okay?"

"Yeah, it's okay. I have to tell you though that I've never been used this way before. I don't know if I've ever done it on purpose, but I feel like maybe I've always been more of the master type of guy. I guess I always told them what to do."

"Well, hell! With the dick that you swing between your legs man, of course you gave the instructions. Every guy is going to listen to you and do as you say so that he doesn't miss out on getting that dick of yours up in his ass – or down his throat, if that's what he's wanting!"

Overhearing what was being said, George then asked Cory, "You said something on the phone about this one having a good sized stick. I guess he must he hung kind of big, long and thick, right?"

"Right you are! You know that dildo that you just took out of him? Well, that damn dildo, almost, could have been molded from his dick. I kid you not, one hell of a nice dick. After you're done back there, he'll fuck you with it as a thank you – if you want."

"If I want? Hell yes, I will want! I haven't seen it yet! But hell, if it's like that dildo, hell yes I want it up in my ass! Hey, Cory, wonder if we should keep him blindfolded while he fucks my ass also, so that he can just wonder for a few days – hum. I wonder if that's the ass that I fucked the other day? I tell you man – the having had sex with a man, and not knowing who that guy was, is a real turn on! Well, to me it is anyway! I just like the idea of some guy running around that has used my ass before, and I would never know that he was the one, even if I was standing there talking face to face with him! The idea that at some time, that guy might have looked at me and thought, 'I've fucked that guy's ass before, and he doesn't even know it,' is damn exciting!"

"Okay Cory. Let's see if we can get any of this big one up in him. Get him in position on top of you. Hang on to him!"

George put the tip of the big dildo up against Mr. Jim's ass and started to push. Jimbo did not make any negative sounds, just a low groan as if to say,

"I feel it, but it's not going anywhere." He didn't sound like he wanted it stopped. His low groan was a pleasant groan. George continued to push and attempted to re-position it so that it would start to slip in.

"I just don't think his ass is ready to be opened up that far, that fast yet," Cory told George. "That damn thing is so damn big that it really takes a long time to get even, kind of, used to it. I think Mr. Jim's ass is going to need just your fingers going in there first and then getting that hole spread opened."

"Yeah, you're right," George agreed. "I guess the boy didn't have any negative feelings about me trying to get that up in his ass though, did he? I didn't hear any really negative sounds, or he is one hell of a good player that knows how to keep his mouth shut. He showed me some real guts in not screaming how he knew he wouldn't be able to take it, when I said I wanted to do it. Your man has got guts man! He has got guts! You have found yourself a real man here, Cory! No wimp here, is there?"

"No George, I heard some sounds, but they were all good sounds. My man's ass likes to be played with, but tonight is the first time that he has found that out for sure! He just didn't know until tonight that he was walking around with a hungry asshole. Not only do I know that it likes to be played with, but I am also very, very, suspicious that the more it gets played with, the rougher and rougher it's going to want its actions. For only being night one, that ass is already acting like it has had years of experience."

"Hey, you know what George! I think I just figured something out. I think the reason Mr. Jim was so damn afraid of getting his ass played with is that, internally, he kind of knew that once it got started, that he was gonna really want it as rough and as hard as he could get it, and he was afraid that he might lose control of what he asks for."

"Is that right?" He turned his head and asked Jimbo.

"I think you're right. I've known for a long time that I really did want some major stuff to happen back there, but I was afraid that what I was thinking about was way too dangerous, and that I could get myself hurt really bad. I had never thought about being played with like this and also being blindfolded at the same time, but shit man, that is just adding to the excitement for me. I mean, the idea of me lying on top of a lover while some other guy plays with my ass is just something that I never, ever imagined. Then hell! Add the blindfold, which is an excitement that I never expected, and I can see now that I have really been, really hungry for something like this."

"Cory, since I'm with you, I know I'm safe. Even though I have no idea who the guy is back there that's about to ram his fist up in my ass, I'm about as excited as I can be. I gotta admit it man, I'm really anxious to really get played with! Without even really knowing what I am asking for, or knowing what is gonna happen to me or my ass, I do feel safe. You guys talking about not letting me see George, so that I won't know who the guy was that fisted me, or that I fucked, is really, really turning me on! That is something else that I had never thought of, but I like the idea of knowing that some guy, one that I might see out on the street, is the same guy that rammed his fist up in me, and I don't even know to say 'Hi' to him. I can imagine what the look on his face at that time could be. And to think that I have fucked an ass, and hell, that ass could be walking down the street right in front of me, and I have no idea that I fucked it, is way too weird. Or maybe, I should say, way too exciting! Hey, I'm really thinking weird stuff, ain't I?"

"No man, no you're not," Cory assured him. "Maybe, finally, you have allowed yourself to think outside of the box, as they say. I think that what you're saying is completely okay. I'm glad that I get to be part of helping you think that way for a change. Okay, shall we tell Mr. George to get with it? You know damn well, that tonight you're gonna be taking a fist, regardless of how damn scared you tried to act earlier. But now here it is! Let's go for it! It's fisting time, man!"

"Let's go for it," replied Jimbo. "Damn I know I want a fist, I wanna know I can take a fist!"

George used his prior experiences and expertise to get Jimbo's ass spread and opened comfortably so that he could get just almost all of his fist up in there. As his knuckles hit the edge of Jimbo's asshole, as with all asses, that is when the real struggle started. Jimbo did grab ahold of Cory and hugged him very tightly! He moaned into Cory's ears a few times, but at no time did he ask for anything to be stopped. Cory hugged Jimbo back when he knew that Jimbo was experiencing some pain and discomfort. George would push, hoping each time to make just a little more progress, and he would also pull his fist back so that he could turn it slightly to see if there was a better position for him to use. A couple of times the change of position was the wrong thing for Jimbo, and George could tell. He would immediately switch back to the former position that seemed to fit better. Jimbo was very well aware of the extensive amount of time that they were using, and also the rather extreme pressures that his ass was feeling. He did know that his ass was getting sore, and had been sore for some time, but he was damned determined that he would not fail in getting a fist – the very first night that he had tired. He felt that if he didn't get it tonight, then he would have passed up the only night when he could really do it, and be able to truthfully say – he did it the first time! He decided that getting a fist up his ass really had been a bigger quest of his than he had ever realized. He knew that most guys simply do not get a fist the first time that they try, and he was wondering just why he was so damned determined to be the different one. What did he expect to do. Run up and down the street carrying a sign that said, 'Look at me! I got fisted my very first time that I tried!' Why was he wanting to be so different than others? Was he looking for that much acceptance from the world that he needed to do the something that almost nobody else has done? He knew that most people never get a fist rammed up their asses! Then, he also knew that the guys that do get fisted, do not usually get it the first time that they let some guy try. So what was he wanting? Why was he so damn anxious to get it the first time? He decided that Cory had been right about him being afraid that once he really got a chance, he just might lose control. He had never been in a position before where he felt safe, if he did lose control. Until tonight, that is. Tonight was his to enjoy. All of the elements had finally come together! His day had finally come. He was finally getting what he had internally been wanting, for a long time, and now he refused to allow this night to pass without getting a fist up in there. 'I will get it, damn it! I will get it! I don't care if they tear my ass apart, I will get a fist up in my ass tonight!'

Because of the amount of working that had been going on, in and around Jimbo's asshole, George was getting a little concerned that perhaps they should be stopping for the night.

Without speaking to Jimbo, he did ask Cory, "Hey man, how's he doing? You know, I've just about done as much back here in his ass, as any guy that I have ever known, has ever taken. And you guys were playing with the dildos before I even got here. I don't want him wishing we hadn't done this. Do you think I should be stopping for the night and do this another night?"

"No!" Jimbo kind of almost screamed into Cory's ear. "Please, please, I still want it tonight! I can take it! My ass is okay! Please ask him to keep trying! I really do want to know that I got it tonight! Please honey, don't let him stop now, please, okay?"

Jimbo's almost of a scream of, 'No,' reminded Cory so very, very strongly of his first attempt of getting a fist that day at the health club. He knew just what Jimbo was going through, and how excited Jimbo was of what was happening. He knew all about Jimbo's wants and desires of getting it the first time. Cory had been there, one day in his life, and now he was with Jimbo, during that one day of his life.

"Hey George, that ass is going to take whatever it takes to get a fist up in there tonight. He doesn't wanna quit! Let's keep going! I'll hang onto him, and you just keep pushing back there. I guess when a guy's mind is that made up, his ass has got to respond. How close do you think you might be? You been getting pretty close?"

"I'm pretty close. But I've had three or four times already when I thought for sure it was gonna fall in. Well, maybe not fall in, but I thought it would go in, and it just didn't. I'm going to make sure I've got plenty of grease down there, and you tell your man to get ready for a sharp pain! I've been trying to avoid any extra pain, but I think this man would be disappointed if he got the fist, and didn't get a big sharp pain with it to know that he just took a fist! So I'm about ready to do it. You guys ready?"

"Oh shit, Jimbo moaned. Oh God! Cory hold me tight! Everything that I've been looking for, but still afraid of is about to happen. Oh crap man! Why in the hell am I begging for this? Oh gawd man! Cory, squeeze me tight! Real tight! Oh, man, tell him I'm ready whenever he is. Oh gawd man! Cory, I'm so damn scared, but man I want that fist! I wanna know I can take it! Let him do me! Tell him to do it! Oh shit man! Oh damn! Do it! Do it!"

"George, I guess you heard that! This man is no boy tonight! He wants a fist, and I guess he wants it bad! He's willing to take the pain! Do him! Shit man! This is really turning me on too! I've never been in a situation like this before. Fist him George! Fist him!"

George grabbed Jimbo's hip with his left hand and squeezed it tightly as if to move the attention to that part of his body instead of his asshole. Then with one very strong movement and one strong push, he pushed his right hand into Jimbo's asshole. Jimbo screamed! He jerked strongly and kept jerking up and down. He grabbed ahold of Cory and hugged his body as tight as he could and kind of cried into his ear, "Oh man, Oh shit man! His hand is in my ass! His hand is in my ass ain't it? I know it's in my ass! I can feel it! Oh shit, I can feel it! Oh shit, that pain! Oh gawd man! Oh man! Oh Cory, I got it! I really did get fisted! Tell him not to move! Tell him to keep it in there for a few minutes. Oh shit man! Oh man! I've really got a guys fist up in my ass! I did it! I did it!"

George took a sigh of relief, and positioned himself so that he could rather lie down on the bed and rest his hand up inside of Jimbo's hot and anxious ass. From his many, many, prior experiences, George knew that he had to keep his hand up inside of the ass once it snapped in. He knew from experience, that, whoever the guy was that was getting fisted, would scream and jerk, and usually yell for him to pull his hand back out. But he knew that pulling it back out that fast, was the wrong thing to do. Jimbo did not yell for him to pull it out – although George did know, that Jimbo was internally, wanting to get that hand back out of his ass! He knew that the initial pain is so sharp, that the only thing the guy getting fisted can think of right then, is – get that damn hand out of my ass! The fact that Jimbo did not yell to get it out, showed just how badly he had really been wanting to get a fist, up in his ass!

Jimbo completely flattened out across Cory and told him, "It doesn't hurt anymore now. It was a real quick and a sharp pain, but it didn't last very long. I could feel my ass grabbing around his wrist! Now I can feel George's hand up in me. Ask George to kind of move his fingers, and wiggle his hand, so I can see what that feels like? I wanna feel his fingers moving up in there! I wanna feel that!"

Cory did not need to ask. George heard the request and did respond.

"Oh shit man, oh damn that feels so good! Oh me! Oh, man! I've never felt anything like that before! Oh man! Oh shit! Oh, I wish I had been getting fisted for a long time now. Oh now I know why guys get fisted! Oh, I always heard other guys say how good it feels to get fisted! Oh shit, they are so right! Oh gawd yeah man, oh yeah! Hey, honey, can you ask George if he can see, if he can maybe push it up in me any farther? I wanna see if I can take more of it up in me. I wanna see if I can! I wanna see if I can do it!"

"Hey, Mr. Jim!" Cory responded, "You are now past the point of no return. You just graduated yourself from a boy toy to a mature man, that has just proven to himself, and to us too, that you love to get another guy's fist up inside of you. So if you're interested in getting your 'fister master' to go into you deeper, his name is Mr. George. If you want more of him up in you, then you need to ask him – yourself."

"Oh, Mr. George! Thank you sir for everything that you are doing! Oh, sir, your hand feels so good in me, sir! Sir, may I ask for more of you, if it's possible? If you can sir, can you stick more of your hand or your arm or whatever, up in me? Please!"

George did reposition himself so that he would be in a better position to force more of his hand up and into Jimbo's chamber. He did make some progress, and did go in far enough, so that he would be able to tell Jimbo later that he had put more than just a hand up into his ass. He had been successful in getting his hand and then probably another two or three inches of his arm up into Jimbo's ass. After that invasion, George patted Jimbo on his bare behind, and congratulated him on his success.

He told Jimbo, "Asshole boy toy, I congratulate you and your ass for what you have succeeded in doing tonight. Boy, you really are a different type of guy! I think there has only been one other guy that took my hand the first time we played, and I do have to admit that maybe that should never have happened. He called me a "M-F" and I got really pissed at him. Some stupid guy, tied down, all fours, with a bare ass up in the air should know better and watch out for what, in the hell, he is calling his fister. So anyway, I am damn proud of you and your asshole for taking what you took tonight without having some raging, pissed off person, doing it to you."

"George," Cory interrupted, "What happened that night? What went on?"

"That simple asshole started getting smart with me and ended up calling me the wrong nasty name while I had him all tied down! I was about ready to ram my baseball bat up in his ass after that! Hey, he learned how to get fisted that night! He sure found out how loud he could scream too! That was what he had asked for, and after he started getting smart assed with me, I decide that he was going to get what he wanted, regardless if he still wanted it now or not! After I got done with him, I asked him if maybe he had learned a lesson about how to treat people that might have something to say about it. He admitted that he had been pretty stupid to do that, and especially since I just let him lie there, all tied up, for about forty five minutes after I got my hand out of him! He kind of changed his attitude after that!"

"Shit man! Do you ever see that guy anymore?" Cory asked with some anxiety and concern.

"Oh yeah! I fist him all of the time now! He's become one of my more regular playmates! He's actually wanted to hire me to fist him, too. He's offered to pay me more than once! I guess maybe he's now glad that he got what he wanted, although maybe he went about it the wrong way! He likes it rough and tough! Only problem is, when he wants it, he wants it right then! That's one of the reasons he offers to pay me for it. He gets horny for it, he needs it right then! Hey, you know those married guys have to be straightened out sometimes! They want it, and they want it right then!"

"Oh, golly, he's a married guy? How in the hell did you find him in the first place?"

"I was out cutting the grass one day, and he came riding by on his bike. I think he probably knew that I lived there by myself. I'd seen him ride by before. Anyway that day, he stopped and we talked. Small shit stuff! Nothing important, and that really made me wonder if something was up. It was! He shifted on his bike seat once, kind of turned toward me and his short silky little gym shorts were showing a big boner. Knowing that he wanted me to see it, I mean, it's hard and sticking out of the end of his shorts, and he then turns it toward me! I just simply asked him if he had a problem going there that needed to be taken care of, in the house. He looked at me, grinned and shook his head, "Yeah!" After we played a few times, is when he found out that I like to fist, and he told me that he wanted me to do him. He said he'd never done that before, but he'd heard about guys doing

it, and he wanted to try it. So we got together later that week and that's
when he got all smart assed with me! Wrong move! But like I said, I guess
I'm the only thing available to him, because he comes over probably at least
once a week and maybe more if he has the time. We usually suck and fuck,
but then there are the times we fist if he's got enough time available."

Looking at George with a broad smile across his face, Cory asked, "George,
how old is this guy? What's he like?"

"Oh he's like about maybe twenty seven or twenty eight. Big built guy!
Said he used to play football in high school, and he's got a dick of death
on him! And damn man, he knows how in the hell to use it! He's a daddy
of three little kids. I know damn well what kind of fun she had getting
pregnant with those kids! So anyway, doing the daddy type of guy, can
be fun, you know! Hell, especially when you don't even have to go out
and look for it! It comes to your house! I see him and his wife around the
neighborhood once in awhile with the kids, and man, it's a total turn on to
me to know that she sure ain't the only one that gets fucked with that big
dick of his! Whenever I see 'em someplace, I get an automatic hardon, just
thinking about him and me in bed together! Damn man – it's hard to keep
secrets – you know? I see them in a store, and I just wanna scream, 'He
fucks me too!'"

During his explanation to Cory about the guy that just about got a baseball
bat rammed up in his ass, and how much fun he has with him now, George
had been rubbing Jimbo's bare ass and ever so slowly moving his hand
around inside of Jimbo's ass. He had been rough with that ass, and the time
had now come for him to be very gentle and loving with it. He leaned down
and kissed both sides of Jimbo's butt and ran his tongue up along the spine
line. Slowly and gently he continued to pull his hand back toward himself.

"Grab your man Cory. I'm about ready to pull my hand back out, and he's
gonna feel it. Give him a hug! Squeeze him, and let him know that he is
now part of the fisting community. He's a totally different man now, than
he was earlier tonight."

George did pull his hand back slowly, as far as he could, before he quickly,
and completely, removed it from inside of Jimbo's asshole.

Jimbo jerked and let out a low moan. Once again he proclaimed, "Oh gawd! That is so damn good! Oh man, I am so glad I got fisted! Oh yeah, I wanted to do that! I wanted to get fisted! Oh man, that feels so damn good! Thank you men! Oh, thank you both, for helping me do that! Oh thank you guys!"

"Okay Cory. Now that we have that hole somewhat trained and experienced, I want to see that dick that you told me about. What do you think about the blindfold? Don't you think he should keep it on him? That way he only knows that some guy played with his dick, sucked on it, and then he fucked the guy in the ass, but he has no idea of what in the hell the guy even looks like. And if he just happens to see him, he won't know it, and besides, he'll be looking at all the guys, wondering if that one happens to be the one?"

"George, I think that is one hell of an idea! I've never had that happen to me – where I either got fucked by some guy, or fucked some guy that I didn't know who he was, or at least knew what he looked like. Yeah, let's keep him blindfolded and just let him wonder."

"Great! I kind of like the idea too of getting fucked by some guy that I have no idea who in the hell he is! Hey, Cory, we need to get our heads together so we can figure out where I can just happen to be – so that he's around me – without him knowing that his fister guy, is right there looking at him, and at his ass! I just think that would be a riot, standing there, looking at him, knowing that I've fisted him, and he's fucked my ass, and he has no idea at all, that I am the guy. Just imagine, maybe standing in line, right in front of him at the grocery store, and I know I've had my hand up in his ass, and he's fucked my ass, and he has no idea of who in the hell I am! Or, maybe standing, on a street corner, waiting on traffic. I'm standing there remembering how I pushed my hand up in that ass, and his big dick down in my ass, or maybe down in my throat, and he doesn't even know to say 'Hello!' Damn, I like that!"

Cory rolled Jimbo off to the side and told Jimbo, "Okay man. You are now going to get sucked on by a stranger, and then you are going to fuck that stranger. Okay? You ready for this, man? You ain't gonna know what he looks like, but you're gonna have some good hot sex with him. He's already fisted your ass, and now he's gonna suck on you, and then you're gonna fuck his ass! Okay? Got it man, got it?""

Although he was asked if this was okay, Jimbo had kind of found out that his opinions and thoughts were not really too important tonight. Neither man had asked him if this secret idea was okay with him or not. Jimbo thought, 'Nobody has asked me if I want any part of this or not, but I guess I'm kind of glad – because I wonder if it's really kind of weird to really like it, and get turned on with the idea of not knowing who you have just had sex with. It's a real big turn on to me, and I don't even have to admit that. I'll just play along. But, yeah this is going to be the first time I've ever had sex with somebody that I couldn't name in a line up – that is if I had to. Fuck man, I like this! I feel like I'm really being used! I like this idea! I like the idea of not knowing who in the hell this guy is! This is a fucking turn on to me!'

George rather looked at Jimbo's dick and then looked at Cory, as if to say, "Are you shitting me? Holy shit man! This is one hell of a nice dick!"

Then George did ask. "Does this thing get bigger and bigger when it gets sucked on?"

"George, just take that little hot dog in your mouth, and start sucking, okay?"

As George did start sucking, things did start to happen, and very quickly! George pulled off of it and looking at Cory, exclaimed! "Oh my God man! Where in the hell was he keeping all of this? I thought it looked good before it got real hard, but shit man – where in the hell did he hide all of this before it got hard?"

George continued to suck and Cory could tell by just standing back and watching, that George was getting damned excited with the meat toy he had in his mouth.

George pulled off of it for a second and turned to Cory. "Have you sucked this thing all the way down? For God sake man, this thing can choke a fucking horse! I have got to get this up in my ass, and I need it now! Give me some grease – quick!"

George slapped some lube on Jimbo's dick and then sat down on it. When he sat down on it so quickly and without any hesitation at all, Jimbo did know that he had a man sitting on his dick, that loved to be fisted! He knew that to be able to sit down on his dick that fast, it took a man that loves to get his ass fisted!

George bounced up and down on it a few times, then pulled off of it and told Jimbo to, 'Lie on top of me. Get that dick up in me. Push that dick up inside of me! Man, I've got to get fucked as hard as possible with that damn thing! Cory, help him get on top of me! Oh man, fuck the hell out of me! Shit, if I had known earlier this thing was in the room, we would've been fucking instead of fisting! Shit this feels good!"

Jimbo fucked George's ass as Cory reached forward and squeezed Jimbo's tits. George acted like this was the first dick that he had ever had up in his ass. He got all excited like some guy does, that is getting sex for his very first time. Jimbo realized that "Mr. George" was getting an experience that he had not recently experienced. Jimbo felt like maybe he was kind of paying "Mr. George" back a little, for the great experience that he had given to Jimbo just a few moments earlier, in the same bed, but in a rather different position!

It didn't take long for Jimbo to reach the point of getting real close to a climax, and as he did, he told George, "I'm sorry man, but I'm about ready to shoot a load and I've gotta pull out of your ass, Oh shit! Oh man! Oh damn that feels so fucking good!"

Jimbo pulled out just a split second or two before the warm explosion of his dick squirted all over George's back.

"Oh shit man!" George said. "We've gotta buy some of those horse condoms that they use on horses to collect horse sperm. That's probably about the size of condom we'll need to buy to get one on you, so that you can stay in there the next time you shoot. I sure as hell hope that the two of you like the idea of us doing three ways in the future. I want to fist the two of you at the same time while you're hugging each other, and as pay back, I want that dick up in my ass for as long as possible. Is that okay with you guys?"

Jimbo informed him that if he buys the "larger size" condoms, they do fit, he really doesn't need the horse condoms, but yeah, he has found out that the normal size condom is too small, and he can't get 'em to unroll on his dick. He apologized that he didn't have one on during that session, but if he ever found out exactly just who he was, then he'd definitely would invite him back sometime to get another fucking. And he really did like the idea of he and Cory getting fisted at the same time, as they hugged each other. He told George that he really did like that idea!

Jimbo told George, "Man with the idea of the double fisting, you have just assured yourself of another fucking from me!"

With that comment, and that anticipation of the next fucking, George told Cory that keeping the secret maybe wasn't such a good thing after all.

Cory laughed and told George, "No man. I think right now the secret thing is a good thing! I think we'll stick with it for tonight! But yes, with the idea of the double fisting, I'm sure the secret will not be kept for too long. I like the idea of the two of us getting fisted at the same time, so I'm sure I'll be letting the cat out of the bag, pretty soon."

"Now, Mr. George, you go get cleaned up and get the hell out of here, so I can take Mr. Jim's blindfold off."

After George did get washed up and got re-dressed, all three men did hug, although Jimbo still was not allowed to remove his blindfold, and Cory and Jimbo thanked George very strongly for his help and all of the activity that night.

Jimbo laughingly told George, "Okay man! Now, if you just happen to read in the newspaper about some guy going up to guys, and asking them if they happen to be the one that fisted him, you might want to let the police know that you are the one."

"Oh yeah, man. I can just see you walking around saying , 'Let me feel your hand. Now, let me feel your butt. Yeah, I think you're the guy I played with the other night!' Now that sounds like a national news story. Film at 11!"

After George left, Cory removed Jimbo's blindfold, and asked him how he felt about the, 'not knowing,' aspect of the evening.

"I have to admit to you, that it really turns me on! I have some guy out there that has had his hand up inside of my ass, he has sucked on my dick, and

I have fucked his ass, and I do not know who he is! He could come to the front door as a salesman, or some politician guy, or even maybe as a driver to the construction site, and I wouldn't know that he and I have had sex! Man – that is a complete turn on to me! Yeah, I like that! It's hot! I'll be looking at all kinds of guys just wondering if he's the one or not!"

After checking the house once again, doing the bathroom stuff – soaping each other up, enjoying all of the secret and private spots of each other, the new couple grabbed a quick snack, headed for the bedroom, and Cory asked Jimbo how he thought the night went.

"How in the hell do you think I think it went? I went into this evening kind of like a little boy, and now I feel like I have completely grown up! Yeah, you were so right! I was so damn scared of getting fisted, 'cause I knew that once I got stared on something like that, that I really wanted to go at it as fast and as furious as possible! I knew that just "kind of playing," was not going to make it for me, and yet I had never been with anybody that I really felt like I could totally trust – until you and I got together."

"I have now been fisted, and I feel like I am one of the big boys now! Now I do feel like I can belong with you at the Calf's Skin. Now, I'll feel like I can hold my own with those big guys over there. Hell, I'll bet I probably experienced more tonight than most of them ever have. How many of them have ever had a lover hold 'em and hug 'em when something like that is happening back there, in their ass? I think tonight went great! I just wonder who that guy is that fisted me, though! I do know his name is George, and I know he's tall. That's gonna be fun thinking about for awhile. Just looking at guys, wondering – could that be him? Shit, never thought that would ever happen to me! Hey, Hon, what do you think about tonight?"

"I personally think it was great! I'm so damn glad that you're an ass whore too! When we met, I was so afraid that even though you looked hot as hell – built like a brick shit house – had a personality that anybody would fall for, and of course, then when I found out that you have a dick that is really bigger than any man should have, I was so afraid that maybe you couldn't get wild in the playroom. Get wild like I like to, anyway! I think our days ahead are gonna be some of the wildest days that any two guys could ever hope for. I do!"

"I think tonight – well – hell, the entire weekend went damn well! I know I shouldn't be the one that's really tired, but, I'm smart enough to know that getting fisted is a little more exhausting than just lying there. I guess that's why I feel completely exhausted right now. We've got some normal working lives that we need to live tomorrow. We need to get some sleep!"

"Goodnight honey! Oh, hey! If you just happen to be the guy going up the ladder first tomorrow, ask the guy behind you if your ass looks any different than it used to. If he says something like, 'Yeah man! It does look kinda different,' you just might find a new playmate for us! Hey, Hon, make sure I'm up before you leave – okay?" Cory told Jimbo. "Goodnight babe, I really, really do love you, and man, I love the way you like to play!"

"Goodnight love! Thank you for helping me grow up. I'll make sure you're up before I leave in the morning, and it might be in more than one way! Goodnight Honey – and I really do love you too! To whoever it is 'up there,' that made us meet, thank you so much! What a great weekend! I am so damn happy! Thank God for all of this!"

Each man gave his new partner, probably the strongest and longest kiss that they had shared yet. They then gave each other a very strong hug, another quick kiss, and then snuggled down, body to body, with their arms and legs intertwined for a good, and well deserved, night of sleep.

They both knew that they were about to enter into a completely new, and exciting, loving life – when the alarm clock goes off, on the first Monday morning of life together!

CHAPTER 10

A New Day, A New Man, and A New Life

Jimbo awoke – feeling like it was earlier than usual. He partly sat up, looked around, and finally realized that he was not "at home," in his usual bed. It took just a moment or two for him to realize that this was the first day of his "new life." Nothing was the same. Everything was new! He jokingly thought, "I'm not in Kansas anymore."

This was now Monday morning and it was less than two days ago that he was a single guy, no real love in his life, and no great enjoyments to look forward to. But what a difference a week-end makes.

As he shook his head, trying to completely come awake, he turned to his left and broke a broad smile as he looked at the new, "love of his life," Cory, and started remembering the wild, outrageous and unbelievable week-end that he had just had.

Jimbo looked at the clock, and attempted to figure out if – he was up kind of early – right on time – or should he really "get with it," so that he's not too late getting to work.

"I set the clock, I think!" He thought to himself. "Yeah, I think I set it for about 5:45, so I guess I'm not late. It hasn't gone off yet."

Jimbo reached over to the clock to turn it off so that it would not ring, and while doing so, he realized that it was only about a quarter after five. "No wonder it's not very bright outside," he thought.

Still sitting up, Jimbo had a lot running through his head, and he felt like he was trying to sort it all out, and remember it all – all at once. He was trying to figure out if he should or could just let loose with one great big scream of excitement about the new life, or if he should be quiet and not disturb Cory so that Cory could get his full night's sleep. Well, as full of a night's sleep as possible. Jimbo remembered that after the activity that had happened in that bed the night before, and the time when they finally went to sleep, it really was not possible for either one of them to get a complete night's sleep, unless they slept in for about another four hours or so. Trying to remember back to what he had figured out the night before, he started working it backwards. 'I need to be on the construction site before 7 AM. I've never driven there – at his time of day, from Leaf Lane – but I figure I'll need about 30 or 40 minutes, so that means I need to leave the house by about 6:20. If I need 20 or 30 minutes to take a shower and do all of the bathroom stuff, plus grab a quick cup of coffee and maybe a slice of toast, then I need to be getting active by about a quarter till six. I think that works,' he thought to himself.

Now he felt like he truly did have a big dilemma on his hands to deal with. Can he grab Cory and give him some mad passionate hugs and kisses and tell him how damn happy he is that he chased those tight, form fitting, 501s on Saturday morning, or should he let him sleep and reset the clock so that it'll go off at 7:00, like they had decided last night to do. Oh the dilemma! Oh the dilemma! Oh, how he wanted to just grab him and hug and kiss him! "Damn, tomorrow I'll let him sleep, but today I am getting him up!"

As he slightly fell over onto the top of Cory, he so very gently said, "Hey, Hon, are you awake?"

Cory shifted, kind of turned over toward Jimbo and so very softly and very gently whispered into Jimbo's ear, "Get off of me big man. I don't want you to think that I will be getting up early for you every day, so I can't do it today, or you will expect it every day."

Jimbo knew that was a joke, for two reasons. They had joked the day before about how Cory had declared that he would not be getting up early to fix Jimbo his breakfast every morning, and the tone of his voice had much more laughter in it than any serious tone.

With that comment whispered into his ear, Jimbo then threw his entire body across Cory's and jokingly started jerking up and down on Cory, acting as if they were in the middle of having a wild sex session, and said, "Hey man – remember how I told you that I have to have sex every morning or I simply cannot go to work? Remember that was part of our agreement, that I would live with you and you could take care of all of my needs and fix me food and do my laundry and all of that stuff for me, as long as I got to fuck you every morning! Remember? Remember?"

"Yeah, right!" Cory replied, as he grabbed Jimmy around the chest and hugged as tightly as he could. "You are only here to be taken care of? I don't think so, man! What about the fact that I'm about the only one with a hole big enough and hungry enough to take that dick of yours, and without me, you can't get any sex. Hey – uh? How about those apples, my man? Remember how you told me that you had to be with me because I was the only man that you have found that can let you fuck like a horse, can make me squeal like a pig and roar like a lion. See without me, what are you? One horny, damn big long hung, stud, doing without! Right??"

"Yeah right man! I guess I kind of forgot that we became a team only because, number one, I've got a dick that nobody but you can take, and number two, you've got an ass hole that nobody can fill but me! Right?"

"Oh!" Cory chuckled back. "I wondered why we got together. I never thought about those reasons, but, hey man – I think you are closer to the truth about that number one and number two than maybe you realize."

Cory and Jimbo snuggled up close to each other, gave each other a big hug, about three or four kisses and Jimbo then said, "You know man. When I woke up this morning I had a little trouble trying to figure out just where in the hell I was at. I got real confused as I was trying to wake up. But then when I started coming to my senses and started remembering just where I was, I got so damn excited all over again. Shit, I wish I did not have to go to work today. Saturday afternoon and Sunday was so damn much fun for me, I want every day to be like that!"

"Jimbo man, you sure as hell are not the only one feeling that way. You know we talked a lot about the funny "super natural powers" that seemed to control our getting together, and every time I take my eyes off of you I wonder if – when I look at you again – will I be as excited as I was before – and damn man – I get more excited every time I even think about it."

"Well right now, all I can think about is to say, thank God for those tight 501s and that street construction over on Willard Street last Saturday morning. I'm never buying any more Lottery tickets, man!"

"What? Jimbo, what in the hell are you saying? What does Lottery tickets have to do with our meeting? What are your talking about?"

"Well, the way I see it, I used up all of my good luck Saturday morning, and after everything that clicked so well, and right on time, I do think I have used up all of my good luck, for awhile, at least!"

"I don't know man," Cory laughed. "Your mind is so weird, I hope I can keep up with you! God man! You are not the only lucky guy here, you know that, don't you? When I handed you that other jacket and told you to try it on, shit man, what if I had been wrong and you were some straight guy that got really pissed? Shit man my ass would have been in big trouble!"

"Shit man, your ass is in big trouble! Well, maybe not! I forgot how rough it likes to be fucked, so I guess it would take a lot to get it in trouble, wouldn't it?"

"Hey speaking about asses, how does yours feel today after George had his hand up in there?"

"Oh crap! Cory, I forgot about that! Well, I guess it feels pretty good if I forgot that it got fisted last night! Shit man! You would think that for getting a man's hand up in my ass for the first time, that I would not "kind of" forget about it right away, should I? Cory, I guess there has just been so much new and exciting stuff going on for us this past couple of days, that I'm having trouble remembering all of it. Shit, a hand up in my ass and I forgot? Now that will have to be a secret between just you and me, okay? For God sake don't tell George I forgot. That would not be very complementary to tell him! Oh man! I had so much fun – I forgot about it right away? Crap man, that's pretty damn stupid, aint it?"

"Don't worry, I'll keep my mouth shut about that. But Jimbo my man – when you are climbing those ladders on the job today in front of other guys, you had better make sure there is no wind blowing, or your open ass hole just might make a whistling sound."

"Yeah, I know. You know, I know I am going to have a funny day on the job today."

"Why – why do you think so?"

"Well it's not everyday that I walk around with a shitty ass grin on my face like I know I will be doing today. Oh – and Mark! Hey, after running into him in the bar, and him finding out about me, you know he is going to want to talk and find out everything that is going on, and then I'm wondering if Dad is going to say anything to anybody about my "new" boyfriend?"

Jimbo's Dad is Project Manager at the Hallbrook Homes Construction Company, (the family company that Jimbo is a member of), his brother Bob is the company controller and brother Dick is the sales manager. Jimbo's Dad is on the construction site, but the brothers are at the corporate office, most of the time, that is. They do show up on the construction site once in awhile, but not often enough for Jimbo to be concerned about them today.

"Well, if he does, is there any harm in that? Yesterday at the cookout, he and everybody else all seemed to be glad we are together and I guess they all kind of liked me! I really don't think he will say anything wrong, do you?"

"No, I'm sure he won't. I just don't particularly like being the center of attention, and if anything is said, then that is what happens."

"Well, hey – remember what Mark told you, while we were talking to him the other night, about that other guy that has been trying to come on to you and can't figure you out yet. He might be a fun one to start "getting" back at. You can start playing up to him, without letting him know what is going on, and see what actions you can get him to do. I think your day'll be – all, okay."

"Yeah, I think you are right. Yeah, Clay! Yeah – I need to try getting back at him some for the stuff that he's been doing to me. Damn, I cannot believe he was doing all of that stuff and I never figured it out. I'm sure glad Mark filled me in. Now it will be my turn to see what I can do, and try to keep Clay off balance so that he still does not know for sure if I am gay or not! Damn, Cory, this – I am looking forward to this! Shit, I've got to come up with some good stuff for him."

"I think you will. I have faith in you and Mark getting something put together. I know I professed yesterday that there was no way that I was going to get trapped into getting up early every morning to fix you breakfast, but hey – today is not everyday, and today is kind of a special day. You get showered and dressed and I'm going out and fix you some bacon and eggs so that you have a good start in your day. Okay? And besides that, you had better get off of me, or you will not get any breakfast, and you will be very late getting to work too! Fact is, you might even miss lunch, too!"

"I know. I know. I was lying here just wishing that today was some kind of a holiday or a week-end day or something just so that I could stay here and not have to get up and leave. Yeah – I'm sure that if I failed to show up today, then Dad really would have a lot of questions about where in the hell was I, and what was I doing. Guess you are right, I'd better get up."

Jimbo showered and dressed, and Cory had just enough time to get a good full nutritional breakfast ready as Jimbo came into the kitchen.

"Wow!" Cory exclaimed. "Damn! I'm ready to switch over to construction if I can wear shorts like that and look as damn hot as you do. Shit man. Is that the way you look everyday at work?"

"Well, until it gets a little cooler outside." Jimbo replied. "Then we switch to pants and long sleeve shirts, but while it's still warm out, it's now shorts or cut-offs and T-shirts since I got the company to change their "dress code.""

I'm serious, it really is a lot more comfortable and easier to move wearing shorts than having to wear long pants all of the time."

"Yeah, I can understand, but shit man! How in the hell can I feel comfortable with you running around all day in front of those other construction guys with you looking that damn hot. Shit man, with something like that running around on construction sites, maybe some people are right. Maybe straight guys do just make a choice to be gay. Hell man, if I was a straight guy and saw that coming close to me, I think I'd be ready to make a choice too."

"Okay man, okay! I'm hot! I'm a stud! I'm a hunk! And if I'm all that, then why in the hell don't I get pulled into the construction trailer each day and stripped of my clothes and ravaged with rambunctious sex?"

"Well from what I've heard, Clay tried that one day with you when he supposedly dropped the pencil on the floor, but you didn't respond."

"Yeah, I know. I guess I could have had it that day if I'd have been a little more aware of what was going on, couldn't I?"

"Well, from what Mark said, Clay was really trying to see if you would grab him, but you passed it by, so – what can I say?"

"I guess what you could say is – Jimbo my poor man! Men are making plays for you – and you are not paying attention."

"But hey honey, I guess that's better for you then, ain't it? If I'm too damn dense to realize when someone is after me, then there is not too much chance of me getting it from somewhere else, is there?"

"Right babe! And right now that is good for me, especially after seeing those cut-offs on you!"

As Cory and Jimbo ate breakfast, they continued to sort out their upcoming day. Jimbo's work day is seven to four, or something close to it, and Cory's day is more like eight to five. Since Cory's drive to work is only a ten minute drive and Jimmy's is more like a forty to forty five minute drive that time of day, it sounded like the two should be coming home at about the same time, or at least pretty close. Cory verified with Jimbo that he did have the house key that they had made for him the day before. Jimbo grabbed his lunch box and his coffee thermos, and headed out the door, after giving his man Cory, a very big hug and a kiss and once again telling him how excited and happy he was about the two of them finding each other.

Cory stood at the garage door and watched as Jimbo headed down Leaf Lane, and headed off for work. Waving, Cory silently mouthed, "I love you man!"

Cory was up earlier than usual since he had gotten up to see Jimbo off to work, so he decided that he could use this additional time to kind of get part of the house a little more arranged for the two living there now, as opposed to the single person that had been its only resident. As he stood in the kitchen, he decided that some moving of the "stuff" in that room could be done so that it worked better for two people to both work in there together, and to eat at the kitchen table when they wished. "Hmmmm –work at the kitchen counter?" He thought about that for a moment. "Saturday and Sunday, we did not eat here at the house except for breakfast, which I fixed. I wonder if he cooks? Oh, I guess there are going to be a number, a big number, of things that I realize I do not yet know about Jimbo! I never thought to even ask if he cooks or not. Hmmmm – well I guess I will find out – won't I?"

Cory decided to just let the kitchen go for the time being. He decided that he really needed to find out if there was going to be two cooks in the family that would be working in the kitchen together, or was re-arranging the "stuff" really of no concern. "If he doesn't cook, I wonder if he likes washing dishes?"

As he walked through the house, he looked at the arrangement in the living room and decided that he really did not have the couch and the chairs arranged for a very workable conversation grouping. As he started to move a chair, he then stopped and thought to himself, "No, don't do this. Jimbo and I need to do some re-arranging of our lives together, and I think we could and should do this together so that he feels like he has been a part of it, and I'm not dictating how everything is going to be." He put the chair back.

"Clothes, yeah, clothes. Jimbo doesn't have very much over here yet, and when he brings more clothes over here, he doesn't have any place to put 'em. Yeah, that's what I can do. I'll make some space for him in the closet and in the dresser. That's something that I can do that will need to be done, but at least if I do that today, then it will show him that I'm anxious to get our lives together." Cory attacked the bedroom clothes closet and quickly moved some shirts, socks, briefs and other small dresser stuff around so that he had made some space for Jimbo. This took a little longer than he expected it to. He then had to rush to get ready for, and to get to work on time.

Jimbo's day on the job site started just a few minutes earlier than usual since his driving time was not quite as long as he had thought it might be. He had given himself about forty minutes from garage to job, but he got there about fifteen minutes early, so he decided that he really didn't need that much driving time and the maybe leaving about thirty minutes early would work. He was in the construction trailer getting some prints when he saw Mark drive in. He went outside and met Mark in the driveway area of the parking lot.

"Hey, good morning Mark. How're you doing?"

"Hey, Jimmy, good morning! Every things good with me – how are you doing?"

"I'm doing great! Hey, I haven't seen Clay around here yet, and when he gets here, remember we are not going to let him know yet that we saw each other at the Calf's Skin Bar, the other night, right? Okay?"

"No Jimmy, that's fine with me. I want to see what kind of crappy stuff we can think up to do to him before we finally let him know you are gay. Now that I know for sure, I'm really going to enjoy being part of this. I think he's got some 'getting back at him' coming first. We've got to see what we can come up with first."

"We'll come up with some good shit, I'm sure! I've got an idea that we might try later this afternoon, if everything works out alright. But, you just let me know about any ideas you come up with! Okay?"

"Yeah, Jimmy, I will. I'll let you know."

"Oh hey, one other thing that I need your help on too, if you will. I'm going to try getting everybody to start calling me Jimbo instead of Jimmy. Cory said he thinks Jimmy is too juvenile, and we decided on "Jimbo." Now don't mention Cory to, or in front of Clay, or he will know the "real me," but I've already told my Dad that I'm switching over to Jimbo, as soon as I can, so when you hear that, that's what's happening. If anybody asks, I'm just going to tell them that I just want to be called Jimbo now, and not explain anything, Okay? Can you help me out there, man?"

"Yeah, sure Jimmy, errrrr – I mean Jimbo. Yeah, I say I'll help – and the very first time, I screw it up. Hey, I guess I only know how to swing a hammer! I'll do my best. Talk to you later, got to get up on that roof and get that thing done. Later man!"

Cory's day on the job was a little more different than Jimbo's was. Cory's co-worker Billy, that they had talked to Sunday afternoon at the Calf's Skin Bar, was standing in the open office area with a nice 'manly looking" bouquet of flowers and a large hand printed sign that read, "Congratulations Our Man, Cory!" They quickly organized a warm greeting and cheers as Cory entered the area.

As Cory rounded the corner and came within view of the grouping, they started clapping and just yelling an unorganized cheer of things like, "Cory, he's our man," or maybe, "Yeah Cory," or "Congratulations." Nobody seemed to be yelling the same thing.

Cory stopped dead in his tracks. It took the "finding Billy" in the middle of the group to realize just what was happening. Then somebody from the group yelled, "Speech man, speech!"

Shaking his head in somewhat of disbelief, Cory took a very big deep breath and responded to the yelled, 'Speech,' request.

"Well, all I can say is, I sure do hope we can repair computers as well as we can really throw somebody for a complete and total loop! I know Billy has to be behind all of this, since he is the only one that knows, or maybe I should say, did know. Now I know why about five people all had stuff for me – that I just had to do right then – for 'em, before I even got into the office. Just when did all of this get organized?"

"And this is not all, sir!" Billy said, as about four people all moved away from a table and exposed a whole table full of kitchen and house type items that were on the table.

"Being the new 'wifey' in the company, we all felt that you might need some wifey type stuff so that you can be the good little ole wife! May we present you with – dish soap, a dust rag, a dish towel, some table polish, glass cleaner, a dust pan, and oh yes, maybe the most important thing on the table, a twenty-four pack of toilet paper! All items that a lady needs in the house!"

Shaking his head, Cory looked at the group, smiled and said, "Well, about all I can say right now is that I certainly did not know that everybody was so damn anxious for me to finally find somebody. My God! If everybody was so anxious, why weren't you all finding me some boyfriends?"

"Cory," Billy responded, "if you will think back, I think you have probably been introduced to about maybe ten or twelve guys that these great folks from our great company introduced you to, but they just were not quite right for you. So we decide that "someday," when that would be, we decided we'd never know, but yet someday we knew you would find somebody. And this weekend seems to finally be the day! After I talked to you and the new guy yesterday, I got on the phone and started spreading the word! Jeannie over there is the one that decided that maybe the kitchen stuff would be fun, so if you've got any complains about already being referred to as the "lady" of the house, she's the one to go get!"

"No, no – I've got no regrets at all! I just can't believe, though, that I happen to work with such a great group of people. How many other gay guys get treated this well from their co-workers? This is way too much to handle and I thank each and everyone of you! Thank you so much! Oh, and I must say a special thanks to whoever brought the toilet bowl cleaner that I see on the table, I really do need that! Now I won't have to stop at the store on the way home! Oh – and the "new guy," as Billy referred to him, is actually Jimbo Hallbrook. Hey, does the name Hallbrook sound familiar to anybody? Like maybe Hallbrook Homes? I see a new home in my future! No – took him first – then found out what his last name was! Took a little figuring out, but finally put the name thing together and asked him if it was the same. It was! Sorry, he is not a multi-millionaire. I will still be working. Damn it!

No, no. Would never leave a great group like all of you. Thank you so very much. Love each and every one of you!"

Mr. Stricker, the manager for the group that Cory works with, stepped to the front of the group and announced, "Well gang! This has been fun. I've been kind of negligent this year by not getting a division party planned and organized, and this has kind of put me in the mood. If everybody and their families can be available this Saturday afternoon, Julia and I would like to have a pool and cookout party at the house. Cory, can you and your man be there so that everybody can meet him?"

"Yeah, I'm sure we can. Well, anyway I'm going to say yes. Yeah, I'm going to say yes, but I'll give him a call in a few minutes just to make sure for certain. But I really doubt that there is a problem." Then as Cory turned toward one of his lady co-workers, with a grin on his face, he kind of lowly said, "I guess there's a lot I need to find out about my man, yet, ain't there?"

Mr. Stricker then said, "Okay gang. Unless Cory gets a negative answer back in a few minutes, everybody at my place Saturday afternoon starting at, about, maybe 2:00 and bring your swim wear if you want to go swimming. That's it, that's all. The company will be furnishing all the rest of the stuff. All of the good stuff. Like the food and drinks. Okay, now I'll go call Julia and tell her that she's having a party Saturday. That should shock her, right?"

Cory called Jimbo's cell phone and had to leave a message asking him to call him back and let him know if there was anything "planned" for Saturday afternoon that he did not happen to know about. In his message he explained very quickly about the "all of a sudden company party cookout, but did not tell him about the impromptu session his group had put on for him that morning. After Jimbo returned the call and confirmed that he had nothing on his personal schedule, Cory and Mr. Stricker let everybody else know that the cookout was a definite for Saturday. Mr. Stricker did let his group know that although his wife had not been involved in the planning, she was, non-the-less, anxious for hosting the cookout.

Later in the afternoon Jimbo called Cory and let him know that he was going to stop by his house, after work, and pick up some additional clothes and he wanted to check on the house to see if everything was okay, so he would be home very quickly after he did that.

Cory got home at about 5:15 and Jimbo pulled in about ten minutes later.

"Hello my man." Jimbo said to Cory as he came in the kitchen door and sat some clothes on the kitchen table.

Cory's smiling and grinning response was, "Hello hunk! How is my sexy man?"

Both men reached out, took ahold of his new partner, and gave his man a hug and a strong, long, kiss.

Cory continued, "So how was your day that you were so concerned about? Everything go Okay?"

"Yeah, I guess I really didn't have too much reason to worry about how it was going to go. It went okay. Oh! Hey! Mark and I have already started our little stuff with Clay."

"What? What did you guys do? What did you do to that poor guy?"

"It was later this afternoon, and I asked Clay if he'd get that pile of crap cleaned up over there and load it on the back of the pick-up, so it can be taken to the trash. Then I told Mark that I wanted to go over some prints with him and see if we have everything on hand that we'll need tomorrow."

"As Mark put down his shovel that he was carrying, he glanced over toward Clay and responded to me, saying, "Okay, I'll be right there.""

"Just at that moment I let out somewhat of a scream and kind of yelled, 'Oh shit! Shit, I spilled my whole damn coke all over me! Damn! Hey Mark, grab those rags and try to wipe up these prints so they don't get too ruined. I've got to get this sticky stuff off of me. Hey Clay! I've got to get these sticky shorts off. I'm gonna use this hose and wash off. I've got some shorts, a jockstrap and a towel in the gym bag in my Jeep. Will you go get them for me while I rinse off?'"

"Clay yelled, 'Uh, yeah,' as he took off running toward my Jeep. I stripped everything off and started spraying himself with the hose, and I rather quietly asked Mark, 'Okay, what's he doing? Keep an eye on him but don't let him know you're watching – okay?'"

"Mark told me, 'Yeah, got it man. He's got the gym bag in his hand. He's opening it. Okay, he's got the shorts in his hand, he's got the towel, now he rummaging through the bag.'"

"I said, 'Okay, tell him I said the jock strap might be in the bottom under some stuff. Tell him I said to kind of dig for it, and he'll find it.'"

"As Mark was telling Clay what I had said, he kept watching to see what was happening. He told me, 'He's digging around in there. Oh – wait a minute! He's kind of just staring. I think he's either looking at the condoms, yeah I just saw him have one in his hand. He put it back. I think he found the butt plug! He's looking at something but not taking it out of the bag.'"

"I told Mark to yell over at him and ask him if he found the strap yet."

"'Hey Clay. Did you find the stuff yet?' Mark yelled to him as if he hadn't seen anything. This whole time, Mark had been "acting" as if he was trying to get the prints dried off, and not let Clay know he has been watching him."

"I quietly asked Mark, 'What's he doing?'"

"Mark said, 'Oh, hey, he's headed this way. Don't say anything.'"

"Then Mark asked Clay, as he came back over to the building area, 'Did you find everything okay? Jimbo is over there, kind of hiding around that corner. He stripped everything off so he could rinse that coke off. Take the stuff to him while I finish up here, okay?"

"Clay told him, 'Yeah, I found everything okay.' Then very quietly added, 'I need to talk to you later, okay?'"

"Mark looked at him and said, 'Yeah, okay. Something wrong? Everything okay?'"

"He said, 'Yeah, everything's okay. I just need to talk to you, but keep it under your hat. Don't say anything to Jimbo, okay?'"

"Mark grinned and turned his face away so that Clay couldn't see the grin, and told him, 'Uh, yeah, whatever you say."

"Clay turned and headed over toward the building where I was still "rinsing" himself off. As Clay came around the corner of the building, he saw me standing there completely nude and bending over toward the spigot, but away from him, turning it off. I had my nude, bare ass shining big and bright – right toward Clay's face! I turned around just enough to see Clay stop, saw him take kind of a deep breath and then he told me, 'Uh, hey, I got your stuff for you. Here's the towel.'"

"I finished turning off the spigot, rather slowly, turned around, full frontal toward Clay, and reached out for the towel. Reaching for the towel, I continued to keep an eye on Clay's eyes to see just where they were looking, and sure enough, they looked right down at my crotch. I didn't intend to have a hard-on, but with just the idea of what slimy little joke I and Mark were in the process of pulling off, and knowing that Clay had made some previous plays toward me, trying to get my attention, and maybe some sexual activity from me, my dick was starting to get a little bit on the hard side. I realized that I'd better cover it pretty quickly or I'd be showing Clay the whole thing and the true size of it, when it gets totally excited. Just right now, I did not intend to let Clay know that being naked in front of him was any kind of a turn on for me. I wanted it to come across as – oh, no big deal! I grabbed the towel and started wiping myself dry. Of course the first area that I just had to wipe, just happened to be my dick and of course, my crotch. That swung my dick back and forth, to the left and to the right for a couple of swings. Clay stood there just a few moments longer than necessary. He then quickly turned and apparently realized that he was not removing himself quite fast enough, and he returned back over to the print table where Mark was still standing."

"Mark told me that as he walked up to Mark, he said, 'Mark, that gym bag has got some interesting stuff in it, and shit man, I just saw Jimbo completely naked! His ass was aimed right up toward my face, and then he wiped his dick and his bag. I think his dick was starting to get hard.'"

"Then acting very surprised, Mark turned to Clay and asked, 'What? What do you mean? What's in there? What's in the gym bag?'"

"Speaking very quietly and trying to act as if he had a legitimate reason to be standing at the print table, Clay told Mark. 'While I was getting his stuff out of that bag, I found a tube of lube, about three or four packages of some Extra Large Size condoms, and I also found a butt plug, and some tit clamps! And I think there was a cock ring strap but I didn't have time enough to check it out for sure. The gym card that was in there I am sure is one for the Muscle Boy Gym down on 2nd Street, and I know the usual guys that usually go there. Mark that gym has a lot of gays that go there! Mark, why in the hell would he have some lube and a butt plug and at least one tit clamp in his gym bag unless he plays around with his butt and his tits? Mark, I really do think now, for sure, that Jimbo is gay!'"

"Mark told him, 'God, Clay! You can't say anything to him about this! He probably forgot that stuff was in there, or maybe he didn't think you'd see any of it, but man you can't let him know you saw it! You've got to wait until he says something, if he really is gay! You've got to remember, us gay guys are always hoping that some hot hunk, that we know, is gay! And, maybe those things don't really mean that he is gay! You've tried some other stuff with him before, trying to find out if he was gay or not, and nothing ever happened, so you've got to admit that maybe, just maybe you are just too hopeful!'"

"Clay told him, 'Yeah, you're right. But damn Mark! I just know in my heart that man is gay. Damn, after seeing what I just saw, I'm just that much more convinced! Mark, I've got to find out some way!'"

"As I came around the corner, Clay, in a much more normal volume said, 'Well, guess I'd better get his stuff cleaned up that I was working on, shouldn't I?' Then he looked at me and asked, 'Did you get all of that coke rinsed off?'"

"I said, 'Yeah, I did Clay. Thanks for getting that stuff out of my Jeep for me. I appreciate that. That coke was just too damn sticky to be running around in, for the rest of the day. You guys don't think anybody saw me over there, all in the bare-butt mode, rinsing off, do you? God, I'd hate for somebody to see that and think we were a bunch of weirdoes or something.

Shit man, if they saw that, they might think we were playing around with each other, or something. Right Clay?'"

"Clay kind of slowly said, 'Yeah – right!' As he turned to go back to his pile of trash, he looked down at my gym shorts and noticed the Muscle Boys Gym logo on 'em. Looking back at me, he asked, 'Muscle Boys Gym. That's the one over on something like about 2nd Street, right?'"

"'Yeah, that's right.' I told him. 'The one over close to the Jeep dealership. That's where I bought my Jeep a couple of years ago.'"

"Then he said, 'Oh, yeah. You like that gym? Is it a good place to work out?'"

"I told him, 'Yeah, it's okay. Nothing too fancy about it. Pretty normal in most ways. It's got a small pool and a hot tub. That's a couple of things I like about it. It's got a little more than some of the other places I know of. It's got a dark, 'cool-down' room too. Someplace where you can go lie down for a few minutes after you've had a good, hard, sweaty, workout. Kind of out of the way though!'"

"He said, 'Yeah, I guess it would be, isn't it?'"

"But then I told him, 'I've got a visitor's pass that you could use someday if you wanna check the place out, but like I said, it's out of the way. I'm not sure it would be convenient for all of the time and I'm not too sure if their normal clientele is exactly what you might expect, but hey, I've had that pass for a long time and have never given it to anybody, so if you want to go with me someday, we can do that.'"

"He looked at me and asked, 'What do you mean about their normal clientele? What about them? Why do you say that?'"

"I told him, 'Well, since the name is the Muscle Boys Gym, I think most people think the place is gonna be all full of big strong muscle boys, but it's not. So anyway, I know some visitors leave, kind of disappointed, since the people there are just ordinary guys. You know, just the normal type of guys. Just guys, just like us!'"

"He said, 'Oh, that's okay. I understand what you mean now! Yeah, guys just like us. Oh, okay! Yeah, I'd like to go with you someday if I could. Have you got two passes? Maybe you, me and Mark could all go together? Could that work?'"

"I said, 'Yeah, we can do that. I'll pick up another pass the next time that I'm in there so that someday, all three of us can go together.'"

"Then as he turned again and walked away, he said, 'Great, I really would like that!'"

"Mark then looked at me, shook his head, and with a face wide grin, and told me, 'Shit man. You are so damn nasty! You have got that guy's balls all pulled up tight, and his shorts, all crammed up in his ass! He told me when you were getting dressed that he saw the lube, the cock ring, the condoms and the butt plug. He is now totally convinced. And then the gym thing! Shit man, he is going to be so damn anxious to go to that gym with you that he is going to split his gut waiting. You do know that you have got to tell him pretty damn soon that you are gay, or he is going to drive me completely crazy! I just know that right now, he is really pissed at himself for mentioning about me going to the gym with the two of you. Now, that means that you have to pick up another pass first. I'm sure he wants to go with you the very next time you go. I'm sure he is wishing now, that he had never mentioned me going."

"I told Mark, 'Yeah, I thought about that too. That's why I told him I will have to get a pass. Hell man, you don't even need a pass down there to take a guest in. All you have to do is sign 'em in. I figured that I am going to have to level with him before we would even have time to go to the gym, so I figured the pass thing was no big deal. I know he is going to drive you up the walls pretty soon though, if we don't clear the air pretty quickly. We pulled a pretty good one this time! Thanks man! You did good! Now I owe you one! We'll let this soak in for a few days, and then level with him somehow. I wanna see what he says to you though, before we tell him how nasty we both were to him today!'"

"Then I told Mark, 'Hey, when you throw those old prints away, don't let him see you doing that. That could create some 'problem questions' about just what in the hell was going on here.'"

"He told me, 'Yeah, will do! This gig went way too smoothly today, to have it all messed up now!'"

"So my man, that was the fun part of my day! Hey! Tell me more about this – all of a sudden – company cookout that you guys are having this Saturday. What's up?"

Cory offered Jimbo a beer and told him to sit down and get ready for a real surprise. As Jimbo picked up his beer and sat down at the kitchen table, Cory picked up the sacks of "kitchen stuff" that his group had given him that morning and totally, and completely, filled Jimbo in as to what his day had been like.

"Hey man! You must have one hell of a great group of people down there that you work with. They must have really been anxious for you to tie up with somebody, right? Like how many are in your group and how many were there this morning?"

"Well there's about eighteen total in our group, and a couple of people are out of town today and tomorrow, so there were probably about fifteen or sixteen people there. Shocked the hell out of me when I finally got in the office. I wondered why people kept bothering me as I was trying to get to the office. I thought – shit man – if they don't stop it, I'm going to be late. I guess now, it wouldn't have been a problem if I was, or not, would it?"

"So anyway, we have a swimming and cookout party to go to Saturday afternoon, and I kind of think you are going to be the center of attraction. Everybody is really anxious to meet you."

"Okay, so are we to bring anything. Is this a pot-luck?"

"No, this is a company sponsored get-together, so we don't need to take anything. Well, that is except our swim trunks since Jim and Julia Stricker have a pool. You'll like them. They are really nice people. They're kind of middle age. Their son and daughter are in high school, so they're not real old people. They are nice and fun to be around, even though he is the boss."

"Cory, you said something about swim wear. What kind of trunks are you going to be taking. What swim wear do you have, briefs or baggy beach trunks?"

"Well, I've got to get some new trunks before then. We had a pool party last year, and I don't wanna wear the same thing again – so I need to get some new trunks. We're going to go visit our buddy David at the Sporting Goods Store and buy ourselves some of the hottest trunks that we can find, okay? You will wear skimpy briefs, won't you?"

"God, I don't know Cory. Is that what you want me to wear? This is a company party. Should we be wearing skimpy trunks?"

"Hell yes man! If we came in anything else, everybody would be wondering what in the hell is going on. Every pool get-together that we've ever had, I've worn the skimpiest trunks I can find. It's become kind of a thing for, 'What is Cory wearing today?' Last year, just for the hell of it, I actually had a really very old fashioned pair of long trunks made for me. The kind, like from back in the gay 90's, and just for the fun of it, I had 'em on over my regular trunks. Of course everybody thought that was a hoot! Maybe that's one of the reasons why they would do something for me like they did today. They know I'm up for the fun stuff. I sure know a lot of offices would have to be very, very, careful about doing something like giving a guy "kitchen stuff" and calling him the new wifey, when he gets together with a new boyfriend. Hey, at our office, I figure have fun! So, anyway, you'll wear something skimpy, right?"

"Hey man, it's your office group and if it doesn't cause any problems, I'm all guts to do it. Has anybody ever kind of made a move at you since you wear skimpy trunks at these get togethers?"

"Yeah – there's another gay guy there besides Billy. The other guy is Brad. I think he kind of got all hot and bothered last year. That was his first time to be at one of the pool parties and after I stripped off my old fashioned swim wear, and got down to just my trunks, he almost would not get away from me. I saw him checking out my crotch a lot! He eluded later that he'd like to maybe go out for a cup of coffee, but I never attempted to follow up on that offer. He really is of no interest to me. I wasn't going to tell you about him. I was going to let you experience him all for yourself. But since we are a couple, I wonder how he'll act this year? I guess we'll find out, won't we? He's one of the two out of town today, so he wasn't there this morning."

"Well babe, it sounds like our social calendar is starting to get kind of filled up. You did remember that yesterday while we were at David and Suzie's she wants us to come over there for dinner Friday night, right?"

"Yeah, I remember, but what time did we decide? Or did we? Unless you know, I'm going to have to call her and find out. Oh, yeah, we'll be seeing David before then anyway because of going to his place to get the new swim trunks! Oh, God. We'll have to keep David in line. He'll be trying to sell us matching trunks! NOT!!!! Oh, and you know what Jimbo? We really need to get over to my Mom and Dad's like pretty quick so they can meet you and not feel like they've been left out. When do you think we should go over there?"

"Well, Hon, I'm not sure. If we're going to go buy new trunks before Friday evening, I guess we're going to have to do that at night sometime. Does David work any nights?"

"Yeah, right! Never thought about that little shopping time problem. The store is open on Wednesday nights till nine. We'll need to go get the trunks on Wednesday night, so maybe we need to go see my folks either tonight or tomorrow night."

"Why don't you give your Mom a call and you two figure out which night we're going over there, and then – go from there. If we need to go over there tonight we can grab ourselves a sandwich someplace so we're not too late, or do it tomorrow. Whatever works. Okay?"

Cory phoned his Mother and had a short conversation. Because of some neighborhood meeting going on that night, they decided that Cory and his "new friend" would come over the next night at about 8:00. Cory's Mom told him that she figured something was going on, since he had not been at their house over the week-end. So she was anxious to get some kind of a call, so she could find out just what was happening.

"Mom has got the same problem of calling my cell phone as your Mom has. She wondered what was going on this weekend, but call me? No way! She just sits there and wonders, I guess. Anyway, she's anxious to meet you. I told her that we'd bring some ice cream to go with the cake she baked today. Oh – hey – I hope you like carrot cake!"

"Yeah – sounds good to me! About the only kind of cake that I really don't like is real dark chocolate. I made myself sick on eating too much chocolate one day when I was a little boy, and so I have trouble with dark chocolate, now."

Cory looked at Jimbo and with a wide grin on his face asked, "Oh chocolate. All chocolate, or just some chocolate?"

Jimmy caught on very quickly about what Cory was actually getting at and replied, " No, no man! Let's not get things all confused here! No problem with THAT kind of chocolate. I got no problem there! I've had some damn good times with THAT kind of chocolate. Just with the kind that I tried to make a complete meal out of one day when I was about seven years old, and made myself really sick. I've done a lot of licking and chewing on the other kind of chocolate, and I have never had any problem there!"

"Okay man. I'm glad to hear that, since I've got a pretty close friend, Edwin, that I want you to get to know too. You know what? I kind of think Edwin is maybe going to be disappointed to hear that you and I have tied up together. He's made a lot of hints that he'd like to see us get together as a couple. He really is a good, fun, guy, but for some reason – I just could never see us as a couple. But hey! You know what I think might be kind of funny right now?"

"No, what?"

"Right now, I kind of think that the main reason that I "just could not" see us as a couple, was because I figured everybody would think I just tied up with him because of his big dick. I didn't want everybody thinking that I just went for the big dick. And now I've got you, and yours is a lot bigger than his is! Shit man! Oh well – that's life! So sorry Edwin!"

"So tell me about Edwin. Feed me the details! Let me know all the dirty gritty stuff about you and Edwin. What's he like?"

"He's hot! Yeah – I don't deny that at all. He is one hot dude. Stands about six foot one or two." Has spent a lot of time in the weight room, and it shows. Met him at the Calf's Skin Bar, so you can imagine he does like to wear leather. And I might add, tight leather. How in the hell he gets it on once in awhile – I really do not know! When he puts leather on, it really looks like it's his own skin! Tight as hell! Fits him like it's painted on! He's about thirty five years old and works in an appliance warehouse. Shit man, I don't think he even uses those two wheel carts they have. I think he just picks up those refrigerators and ovens and stuff and just carries 'em over his head! Big arms! Oh yeah, you know what kind of sexual activity I like – so you can imagine how we met! A couple of guys at the bar knew one day that I was looking for a good fister, and they heard him saying something about how finding a good bottom was so difficult, and so those guys told him they thought maybe, they knew a guy that he should meet. They knew I was in the outside Corral area, so one of 'em came out and got me and took me inside and introduced us. So anyway, later that night, I had a chance to find out just how good of a fister he was, and he had a chance to find out if I was a good bottom to play with or not. I guess I qualified. We've fisted probably about ten or twelve times now since then!"

"Are you always the bottom, or does he let you fist him too?"

"Oh, yeah! He puts his ass up in the air too. He likes both directions. It was just at the time that we met, he was having trouble finding guys to stick his fist up in, at that time. He pulled off a fisting party at his house once that I went to, and he had thirteen guys there. All of 'em ready to do it, and to get it done!"

"Thirteen!? That's an odd number. That doesn't sound like that would work. Somebody is getting left out there!"

"No, he always has an odd number at all of his get togethers. He says there is always one guy that needs to take a break at sometime, and having an odd number means that no second person is sitting around because somebody is not playing. He says it works out well, and the time I was there, it sure did.

Course, you know me. I was never the guy that needed to take a break. I kept yelling, next, next!"

"Shit man, I'll bet you did. So do you and Edwin have any future sessions on the "map" so to say? Anything planned at this time?"

"No, nothing planned. You know usually when we get together it's usually a last minute thing. He'll give me a call or I'll give him a call and if neither one of us is busy, then we do our thing. Are you hoping we have something planned so that you can join in?"

"Hell yes! I think he sounds like fun. I'd love to be part of a three way with him. You, me and him! Hell yes! That sounds great to me! Would you set it up?"

"Yeah, I'll do that. Jimbo, I kind of guess that maybe you and I do kind of have the same type of attitude about having others involved in our sex play. As long as both of us are involved, then doing it or setting up a three way is okay. Right?"

"Hey Hon – as long as you agree with it – I like it. As long as we are both interested in the other guy, I'd kind of like for us to take the opportunity to play with him and use him for our fun! You and I sure do seem to like the same things, and I can know already, that is gonna be one of the main things that makes us love each other so much! And from what you're telling me, I think Edwin sounds like we could have a hell of a lot of fun playing with him together. Since he has multiple guy, fisting sessions – then I guess he's not opposed to doing three ways, right?"

"Oh hell no! He's into just as many guys at one time as he can get together. The way that, I guess you and I both like to play, and the things we both like to do, I think he is gonna fit in with our being together, very well!"

Right then, both men stopped – looked at each other – and without saying a single word, grabbed each other and planted the strongest kiss possible on his mate.

Jimbo then looked at Cory, Cory looked at Jimbo, and almost in a total and complete unison, each man said, "Man – I love you! Thank God we are finally together!"

As Cory continued to hug Jimbo, he replied, "Thank goodness for one hot man that just had to go take a Jeep ride – to nowhere – for no real reason!"

Jimbo hugged Cory and said, "Thank goodness for those, tight ass hugging 501's! And Jimbo my man, I think it's more true now than when you said it the other day, but yes man, this past weekend definitely does show that we have definitely just landed into a whole new relationship, and a whole new life! I love you, I do! I just know we are gonna have one great life together. You and me – for years and years! Don't ever throw those old Levi's away! Even if neither one of us can put 'em on, and I damned well know, that the older we get, there's gonna be no way in hell that we'll ever be able to do anything with 'em, except just look at 'em! But they are now part of us, and they will always be part of us! A REAL part of us! They are what brought us together."

ABOUT THE AUTHOR

Wade Wright

Wade Wright is a semi-retired father of two daughters and four grandchildren. Transplanted many years ago from the state of Ohio, to the Southwest, now living single – well with the exception of his Min Pin puppy, which has been his sole love for the past eight years!

Enjoyed two loving partnerships, both of which ended way before they were supposed to.

Wade Wright is also the author of *Yes, Cops Do It — Oh Yeah; The Two Straight Guys; Apartment 117; In Cemetery Park; Jay, Jake and Jimmy; The Carpet Installer, Totally Unexpected; Marshmallow Cream — and Hard Big Pieces of Chocolate; Family Matters: and sometimes, it just does not matter; Married Men on the Loose*; and also *We Have Just Landed - Volume One;* available from TheNazcaPlainsCorp.com, Amazon.com, or your local bookstore.

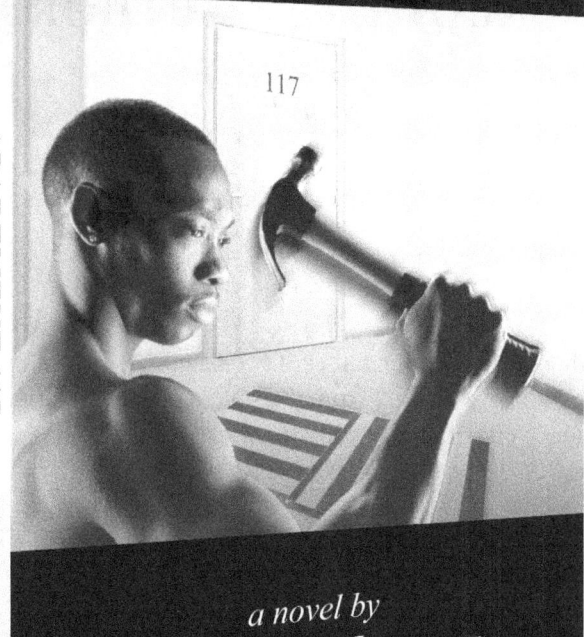

APARTMENT 117

APARTMENT 117

WRIGHT

117

a novel by

WADE WRIGHT

A
BONER
BOOK

FAMILY MATTERS
– and sometimes, it just does not matter

WRIGHT

FAMILY MATTERS

WADE
WRIGHT

A
GOSHER
BOOK

IN CEMETERY PARK

A NOVEL BY
WADE WRIGHT

A BONER BOOK

WRIGHT
JAY, JAKE AND JIMMY
JAY, JAKE
AND JIMMY
A NOVEL BY
WADE WRIGHT

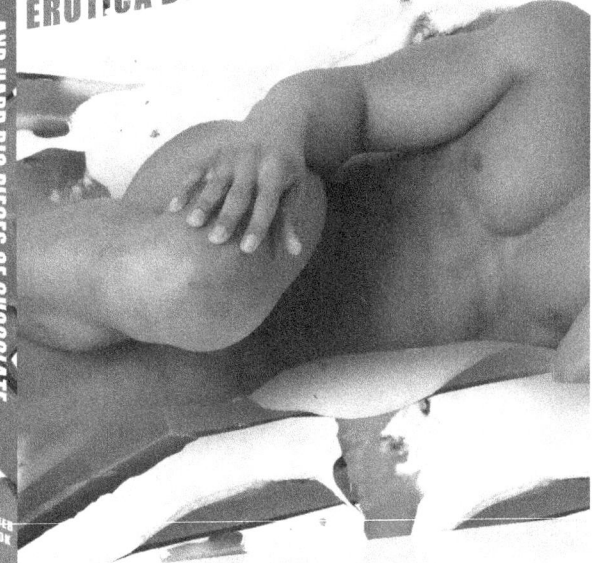

MARSHMALLOW CREAM
– AND HARD BIG PIECES OF CHOCOLATE

EROTICA BY WADE WRIGHT

WRIGHT

MARSHMALLOW CREAM – AND HARD BIG PIECES OF CHOCOLATE

A BONER BOOK

The Carpet Installer

Installer

Wade Wright

A BONER BOOK

The Two Straight Guys

The Two Straight Guys

Wright

a novel by
Wade Wright

A
BONER
BOOK

TOTALLY
UNEXPECTED!

WADE
WRIGHT

A
BOYER
BOOK

WRIGHT
“YES, COPS DO IT, – OH YEAH!”
A BONER BOOK
“YES, COPS DO IT,
– OH YEAH!”
a collection of stories by
WADE WRIGHT

www.ingramcontent.com/pod-product-compliance
Lightning Source LLC
Chambersburg PA
CBHW051132260626
47170CB00005B/1773